PRAISE FOR CASSANDRA L. THOMPSON

"Put on your combat books and take a stroll through Thompson's picture of suburbia, where the trees are pruned and the sidewalks are freshly paved. It won't take long to realize that the sepia toned nostalgia feels a little too heavy, and that every smile of sunny disposition is full of cracks. Behind every door is a visceral story of gore and violence, and *My Little Black Book of Horror* is not just your guide to where the bodies are, but your backstage pass to all the unhinged horror that got them there in the first place."

REBECCA JONES-HOWE, AUTHOR OF VILE MEN & ENDING IN ASHES

"Beware: *This book has teeth*. Tiny teeth, yes—but they are sharp, and they are many. In 17 stories, Cassandra L. Thompson proves herself the queen of the Short Sharp Shock, and leaves horror-lovers of all stripes gasping for air."

JACOB STEVEN MOHR, AUTHOR OF THE UNWELCOME

MY LITTLE BLACK BOOK OF HORROR.

MY LITTLE BLACK BOOK OF HORROR.

CASSANDRA L. THOMPSON

MY LITTLE BLACK BOOK OF HORROR
BY CASSANDRA L. THOMPSON
EDITED BY DAMON BARRET ROE
PUBLISHED BY QUILL & CROW PUBLISHING HOUSE

Cover Design by Cassandra L. Thompson, Fay Lane

Interior by Cassandra L. Thompson

Printed in the United States of America

ISBN (ebook) 978-1-958228-45-6

ISBN (paperbook): 978-1-958228-46-3

Publisher's Website: www.quillandcrowpublishinghouse.com

For Andrew.

***Content warning:** The stories in this book contain scenes of graphic violence and many explore topics that could be triggering for some. For a detailed list, please consult the Trigger Index located in the back of the book.*

TABLE OF CONTENTS.

ICE CREAM.

"THIS HAS BEEN the hike from hell," Jake remarked, stopping to catch his breath and take another gulp of their dwindling water.

Celeste wordlessly agreed, appreciating the moment to rest her aching leg muscles. The sun hung blisteringly high in the sky without a cloud in sight, pulling the temperature up to an arid 85 degrees, perhaps the worst conditions to hike in. Sweat didn't just drip down her back, it poured, leaving her tank and shorts soaked.

If she'd had the energy to chastise Jake for getting them lost in some endless Ohio cornfield, she would have, but for now, she reserved her energy. He was the one who'd insisted they leave their phones behind and find their path 'the old-fashioned way'; he was the one who'd chosen the trail, the one who'd convinced her to take one 'slight deviation' from the main path to avoid the mud since he was 'really good at finding his way.'

"Maybe we should just turn around and follow the path back," she suggested after taking a sip of the bottle he'd tossed to her.

"Turn back and walk for another four hours? I don't think so. We don't have enough water to make it. There's got to be something up ahead past the cornfield."

Celeste sighed. "Yeah, a church filled with children who want to sacrifice us to their corn gods."

Jake put his hands on his hips. "This is a National Park Trail. They will have places to rest. Quit being dramatic—I'm hot too. Let's just go a bit further."

Celeste groaned, pushing her tired body forward despite its aching protestations. She wondered if she was more sensitive to heat since the little purple line on the pregnancy test rudely announced an unexpected arrival. She'd promised herself she wouldn't allow it to alter their lives in any way; she'd be damned if she gave up her exercise routine or her sushi. Today made her wonder if she'd made a mistake.

After some time, shadows moved across the unrelenting sun, and she looked up, hoping to see some white, puffy clouds crossing overhead. She realized it was actually a pair of vultures, patiently soaring in zigzags as they walked. "Jake, we're going to die and get eaten by buzzards."

"Look up ahead," he said, ignoring the comment.

"It's probably a mirage, like on the Looney Tunes. Remember that show? The buzzards circling overhead and the pretend oasis in the desert?"

"It's a damn ice cream shop," Jake realized, elation in his voice. "I told you there would be a pit stop. We can ask them for directions."

"Oh, thank God." Celeste sighed with relief as they found a new burst of energy that pushed them on. The paint on the old white barn was peeling, but the windows looked new enough; the sign in the front of the building that boasted 'Country Trail Ice Cream Shoppe' had another one posted below it that said, OPEN. A few picnic tables were on the side, one with a folded umbrella. Celeste smiled. It had been a long time since she visited such a quaint, old-fashioned ice cream shop.

Jake opened the door to release a blast of orgasmically cold air on their faces. Celeste didn't even have time to worry about how crazy they must look to the shop owners before she closed her eyes and moaned with happiness.

Jake gave her a nudge. She opened her eyes to see a young waif of a teenager with sprinkles of acne and thin, oily blonde hair gathered behind her neck.

"Sorry, we were lost in this awful heat," Celeste said with a smile. "Can we please have some water?"

The teenage girl suddenly looked nervous. "We only have well water here, ma'am. I wouldn't suggest drinking it."

"Well, we're going to have to chance it. We need water."

"Let me go get my manager," she said meekly, disappearing behind the wall.

Jake and Celeste shared a look.

"I think I'll jump over the counter and strangle her if they don't give us some damn water," he told her. His face had taken on the shade of a tomato, and the lips he licked with his dry tongue were equally dry and cracked.

Celeste looked around them, appreciative at least to be in the air conditioning. The counter displayed various flavors of ice cream in vats, and there were several small tables next to the window with silver napkin holders. Her eyes focused on a small fly that buzzed around them, landing on the metal scoop that had been left in a vat of creamy pink. She suddenly tasted the strawberries, and her mouth responded with a gush of saliva.

A booming voice filled the parlor. "Hey there, folks. Sorry for the misunderstanding."

Celeste looked up to see a man in his late forties with a wispy crop of black hair and an even blacker mustache, wearing a cherry-stained apron. He looked abnormally tall next to the teenage girl who had summoned him, who shyly averted her eyes as he spoke.

His large swell of stomach bounced as he talked. "We get our water from the well, but a few days ago, one of our cows found its way in there and drowned. It's an open well, you see, but usually, the cows don't make it that far. Anyways, the old girl tripped and fell in, and no one was the wiser until a few days later when there was a funny taste in the water. We fished her corpse out, but I don't think you'll be wanting to drink any of that for a while."

Jake shared Celeste's look of disgust but tried to maintain his typical pleasant demeanor. "Do you have anything at all to drink? We got lost hiking, and the wife and I are exhausted."

The man suddenly locked in on Celeste with his dark eyes. "Are you having a baby?"

Celeste blinked, surprised. "How did you know? I'm not even showing yet."

The man gave her an abnormally wide grin. "I have a way with these things," he boasted. "All we have here is ice cream, but since you're having a little one and ya'll got yourself lost in the field, I'll give you a scoop on the house."

Celeste sighed with relief. "Oh, thank you," she said, hurrying to the counter. "I'll take the strawberry."

"I'll try the pistachio," Jake said from behind her.

The man hummed as he retrieved two cones from the back. Celeste noticed the girl had disappeared.

"You're both in for a real treat," the man told them as he scooped up the pale green concoction for Jake. "This here is the best ice cream around town, made from the finest cows. We use all local, organic ingredients."

Celeste nodded absently, consumed by thoughts of how wonderful the cool creaminess would feel on her tongue, fantasizing about the rush of sugar on her taste buds.

The man handed Jake his cone, and he promptly took a huge bite off the top. "This is amazing," he groaned. "How do you make it taste so good?"

"Pistachio is my favorite one to make," the man said, placing a strawberry scoop on Celeste's cone with care. "You just grind up the pistachios with a bit of bone meal, then add the sugar and the snake eggs, and of course, the whipping cream and breast milk. You put it all in the grinder, add a drop of green food coloring, and mix it with some ice. Comes out perfect every time."

Jake stopped licking his half-finished cone to stare at him. "I'm sorry—what did you say?"

Celeste was lost in the delectable layered flavors of berries, but the look on her husband's face caused her to snap back to attention.

"Oh, don't tell me you're grossed out by my special ingredients." The man laughed. "Come on now, who doesn't love ice cream? I'm surprised, though. I thought for sure you'd taste the bitter almond on your first lick. I'm a better mixer than I thought."

Celeste suddenly felt light-headed, frozen with shock as Jake dropped his ice cream, the pastel mush hitting the ground with a thud. He grabbed her arm, wrenching her from the parlor and back out the door into the blazing sun. She tried to keep from vomiting as he broke into a sprint, yanking her along. They didn't get very far into the field before he collapsed, foaming at the mouth as he gasped for air.

She fell to her knees, shaking him. "What's happening?" she shrieked at the circling buzzards and a God who did not exist. Then she realized with a horrific jolt: cyanide tastes and smells like bitter almond.

Jake began to convulse, his eyes bulging out of his now purple face, but she heard the man approaching, upsetting the long waves of grass in the field as he lumbered toward her. Sobbing, she kissed Jake on his forehead as he died and bolted, punching back the random corn stalks that branched in her way.

"Aw, come on, now, ma'am, you shouldn't be running in this heat with a baby in there!" the ice cream man called.

She was quite fit, but the hike had drained her, and although she heard him getting closer, she couldn't keep going, her legs buckling beneath her while her head spun. She collapsed, the giant shadow of the man looming over her. "Please," she croaked helplessly.

"I'm really sorry, ma'am, but I've been needing another cow to milk for the ice cream," he told her as he took a minute to catch his breath. "Don't worry about the baby. I do sell the boys up the street to Grayer's for veal, but I put the girls to work in the parlor until they are ready to make milk. I can tell you've got a little girl in that stomach of yours. Don't worry. I take real good care of my cows—plenty of time for leisure and a fenced-in yard that you can play in. Plus, all the ice cream you can eat!"

Celeste couldn't protest, her vision blurring as he crouched down to pick her up, his breath stinking of raw meat. As he hoisted her over his shoulders, she caught sight of the vultures, still circling, and she thought wistfully as her vision faded to black, *I should have just let the buzzards eat me.*

DELIRIUM.

I BELIEVED wellness would come until the day my fingernails fell off, revealing the soft pink of my nail beds, contrasting against my sallow, paper-thin skin. At that point, I no longer cared if I died, my only solace the slip of sunlight peeking out from beneath the curtains at daybreak, whispering empty promises of strolls through the garden and picnics in the countryside.

At first, the loneliness bothered me, the isolation a cruel fist that held me defenseless in its fevered grasp. Fever—that was perhaps the worst of it, my vision, memories, reality slipping through my own fingers like grains of sand. Was I really a mother, a wife, a daughter? Or was I something different, an accursed queen trapped in a tower, waiting for my king to halt the executioner's blade? I longed for a knight to rescue me, staring desperately at the covered window lest I miss his hand. But neither king's order nor dashing chevalier arrived.

Eventually, the maid's visits were few and far between, my chamber pot barely in need of emptying, and the doctors stopped bringing their leeches, though the sores where they suckled still stared at me like hateful eyes. My God, I even missed the leeches. They offered company where there was no longer any company to be had.

At one point, I'd risen, in a pyretic dream perhaps, and threw one of my books at the window, shattering the glass and releasing the cruel winter winds into my room. The pummel of their fists gave me the illusion of vitality, making me feel alive for one glorious moment before I collapsed, snowflakes collecting on my yellowed nightgown.

I awoke to a raven perched on my snow-dusted hip, staring at me with curious black eyes.

"Have you come to collect my soul or my flesh?" I asked her in my mind, no energy to speak aloud. Something wet streamed down my face, but I didn't have to touch it to know it was my blood.

Raven did not respond, just hopped down from her perch towards my slackened fist, examining the empty spaces where my fingernails had been.

"Ah, so it is my flesh," I sighed. "Well, I'd advise against tasting my diseased skin. I have contracted something that frightens all away."

She cocked her head at me, blinking as she studied my eyes.

"Every man who has ever loved me cherished my eyes," I told her. "As you can see, none of them are here. You are more than welcome to them; I shan't be needing them any longer."

A burst of winter air came through the window once more, this one calling my name. I imagined my soul floating along with the sparkling snowflakes, perhaps making it as far as the sea. I watched the vapors of my breath rise to greet them, joining them in their pirouette, following willingly, as we drifted along the spaces between the worlds, over the dead trees and snow-capped hills until the air became brackish and I saw the frothy swirls of endless ocean.

I was there, thankfully, the moment sweet Raven settled her tiny feet on the bridge of my nose, grateful, it seemed, as she helped herself to the soft, warm meal of my useless eyes, eyes the color of the distant sea.

PUSH.

"BILLY!"

He blinked out of his daydream to see his teacher standing above him. Her face always looked like she'd just bitten into a lemon, but it was extra twisted at the moment, a fire in her dumb brown eyes.

She snatched the paper from beneath his arms, the one where he'd been doodling a knife-brandishing Jason surrounded by severed body parts. It was the horror-movie scene he pictured when she first started talking about George Washington. She crumpled the paper in her fist as her lips pressed together so hard they made her face white. She sputtered out short sentences. "Principal. Office. Now."

Billy pretended he was a serial killer being interrogated by the cops as the principal yelled at him. Blank-faced and calm so it would be over quickly. It worked.

The walk home felt too short. Normally, rounding the blocks of shoebox houses to the last one by the fields took forever. He knew his parents would be mad when he showed them the write-up, especially because he'd just pinky-promised his dad he wouldn't draw anything gory at school anymore.

He sighed, slowing his steps.

People didn't understand Billy. He heard adults whisper weird words with stupid meanings behind closed doors and got used to the strange looks when he talked about the things inside his head. He didn't care, though. The world was boring, so he made it fun.

His mom's car wasn't in the driveway when he reached his house, and he silently cheered. She was the one who always demanded to see his folder when he got home from school. His dad was in the kitchen, making dinner. He walked in and tossed his backpack across the table. "My teacher's a bitch," he told his dad. "I'm gonna go play outside."

"Don't swear." His dad turned to see his outfit.

Billy insisted on wearing whatever the hell he wanted to wear, whenever the hell he wanted to wear it, regardless of parental protestations. This morning's outfit had been a big yellow raincoat and rainboots—his Georgie outfit, he called it.

"You do know it's not raining, right?"

"It's part of my costume," Billy informed him. He grabbed a toy knife from the toy box in the hall and his favorite Jason mask out of the pile nearby. It was the one too big for his face, but he decorated it Michael Myers style with markers—not from the old, stupid version of Halloween, the one from the movie his dad let him watch if he promised not to tell Mom.

Billy's backyard was huge, at least an acre, and it ended in an old playground that belonged to his neighbors before they moved. It was rundown, and the swings creaked with rust, making it the perfect setting for his horror movies. He stomped through the high grass toward it, whistling the Halloween theme song now stuck in his head.

The skies were overcast behind the tall trees surrounding him. He imagined them reaching to grab him and the skies pouring rain as he stalked through the grass with his machete, looking for his next kill. He'd decided it was an evil teacher with dumb brown eyes that tortured little kids in her cellar.

He was almost to the playground, where she enticed her victims when he heard someone behind him. He turned around, thinking it was his dad. It was actually a chubby man with tiny glasses wearing a sweat-stained polo.

Billy's movie fell away. He was now just a kid standing in his yard wearing a raincoat, holding a plastic machete from last year's Halloween. He scowled, annoyed that his fantasy was so rudely interrupted.

"Hey, buddy, cool Freddy mask."

Billy just stared, unamused.

"Did you see my dog come through here?"

Billy shook his head. Tiny beads of sweat sat on the man's fleshy forehead, unmoving.

"Can you help me find him? I was supposed to trade in my nephew's XBox for him, but if you help me find my dog, I'll give it to you instead."

Oh, hell no.

"My dad is in the kitchen," Billy warned him.

Billy had fantastic reflexes, but his boots made sprinting difficult—especially in the unmowed grass. Before he knew what was happening, the man had a knife—a real one—pointed at him. "Listen, you little shit," he spat. "You're going to follow me to my car right now, or I will stick this into your guts. Even if you scream, the houses are too far away."

Billy couldn't help it.

He started to giggle.

"You little asshole." The man advanced, drawing close enough that Billy could smell his rotten breath and onion armpits. But he couldn't move the knife any closer. In fact, his arm was frozen in place.

Billy stepped back and removed his mask to get a better view.

The man's arm shook with exertion, his forehead beads now running down the curves of his face. He was turning red like a tomato, making weird grunting sounds as his arm slowly twisted around to point the knife at his own stomach.

A few crow calls cut through the air as they swooped by, the air thickening where they stood.

"What is happening?" the man managed to sputter, his eyes bulging out of their sockets.

Billy didn't respond. He didn't have to use too much energy, but he wanted to stay focused. The man was squishy, malleable like his teacher, Mrs. Hellow. Though Mrs. Hellow didn't deserve to be *pushed* by him. Not yet, anyway.

He watched the man's expression shift from disbelief to terror as the sharp end of his knife went into his shirt. It popped through the thin fabric to his vulnerable flesh, pressing until it pulled crimson to the surface.

"Please, I'm sorry—"

Billy suddenly wondered what his dad was making for dinner. His stomach growled in response. He hoped they'd be able to eat before Mom asked him to produce his backpack. Maybe he could tell them some fat idiot tried to kidnap him, though he doubted they would believe him.

The man screamed when the knife finally slid into

his stomach, back out, and in again until the screams turned into garbled choking. He collapsed like a sack of potatoes, stabbing himself over and over, relentless in his execution. It reminded Billy of when his older cousin used to grab his younger cousin's hand and snack him with it, taunting, "Why are you hitting yourself? Why are you hitting yourself?"

Billy looked down at the barely animated lump of gore. "Why are you stabbing yourself?" he mocked.

The man did not respond.

His arm, coated in what looked like meat sauce, fell with a thud, releasing the knife. Billy waited until the flies came before he was satisfied the man was dead. Then he picked up his Jason mask and headed back across the yard.

He hoped his dad made spaghetti.

B.L.T.

GEORGE WAS A SIMPLE MAN.

He liked burgers, beer, and football. He went to work every day; he paid his taxes. He even made sure to change the oil in his truck before it was due. Life was better lived that way, he surmised, for following routines allowed one to really enjoy the simple pleasures life had to offer. So when he had a hankering for a B.L.T.—just like Mom used to make, with the toasted white bread, the perfectly sliced tomato, and the crispy strips of bacon arranged in a crisscross pattern—he had no problem obliging. He worked in the yard all day, and he deserved a good meal.

"Mom, do we have any lettuce?" he called up to her as he rummaged through the refrigerator. She didn't have to answer because George soon discovered the sopping brown bundle of mush wrapped in plastic. He sighed, realizing he'd have to take a walk up to the store. A B.L.T. was nothing without the lettuce.

It was a warm Saturday, the kind of day right before summer starts when all the trees scatter their blossoms on the street. George was glad he'd brought his baseball cap, the worn blue rim keeping the sun out of his eyes. He was grateful Bob's Corner Store wasn't too far from his house, for although there was a cool breeze drifting through his neighborhood, he felt a few beads of sweat trickle down his temples. He stopped to pull out his handkerchief, dabbing his forehead as he watched one of his neighbors bludgeon the other with a baseball bat, splattering spongy pink on the sidewalk.

He replaced his cap, shoving his handkerchief back into the pocket of his frayed jeans. The walk was working up his appetite—he could almost smell the sizzling bacon in the skillet, almost taste the juicy tomato. He hurried across the crosswalk, sidestepping a bit of roadkill that had attracted a cloud of flies, most of them swarming around the woman's cracked open jaw. He pulled out his wallet, checking to make sure he'd remembered his money. He looked back up to see Bob's door was wide open and untouched, though the Chinese food restaurant across the street was on fire.

George entered, careful not to crunch the broken glass with his work boots because good work boots weren't easy to come by, and headed towards the produce section. He smiled, miraculously finding a head of lettuce that had been left behind. He pulled an unbroken six-pack from the back of the cooler and put them all into the cloth bag he'd kept in his other pocket, leaving a few dollars in Bob's outstretched palm. The bullet wound in his head was attracting its own accumulation of bugs, his syrupy blood still pooling onto the floor.

As soon as he walked outside, a woman crashed into him, eyes bulging out of her sockets as she screamed, "Please, they're killing us!"

George scowled, shoving her away as he turned to

head back down the street. He stopped to check his bag to make sure she hadn't upset his purchases. Satisfied that his produce was unblemished and he wouldn't have to go back and disturb Bob, he continued home just as her screams pummeled the air. They ended with a loud crack as someone smashed her head into the pavement.

He was glad to be away from the riff-raff, squinting up at the sky to see a few clouds covering the sun. They swirled with the plumes of arson smoke that drifted from town.

"Mom, I'm back," he called, making a note to grab some air fresheners for her room the next time he was out. The stink was starting to infiltrate the downstairs. Soon it was replaced with the smell of cooking bacon and toasting bread as George gently sliced the fresh tomato to the perfect thickness. After the bread popped up, he spread a coat of mayo on the top, stacking up the B., the L., and the T. and slicing the tower in half with his kitchen knife. He grabbed a cold one and headed to the living room to watch a recording of the game. Though he was a simple guy, he hated all the commercials and the news broadcasts lately, and recording it let him fast-forward to the good stuff.

He took a bite of the sandwich, letting the delicious combination of juices slide down his throat as he glanced out the window, noticing the bludgeoning neighbor from earlier lying dead in the street, his skin in ribbons. He wondered if he should go out there and grab some fresh meat for later since Mom's would only be good for so long, but he was tired from his walk. He'd never used one that was already dead before, but although she was still alive on all those crazy tubes they put her on, she was running out of edible parts.

He was sure those thugs would be killing each other tomorrow, too. He could make his decision then. It might be nice to stock a couple of thighs and breasts in the fridge for the workweek. He wistfully thought of Mom before she went brain-dead. She used to take care of all that stuff. At least he knew how to duplicate her B.L.T.s.

He took another bite of his sandwich, washing it down with a sip of cold beer before standing up to pull down the blinds and settling back down to watch the game.

SCRATCHES.

"PLEASE MAKE IT STOP SCRATCHING."

The whisper was slurred, disoriented, as if she was still lost in the spiderweb of a dream, breaking through my slumber and prickling the hair on my skin.

I knew if I ignored it, she would stop, and I could go back to pretending I was asleep in my own bed under a pile of warm blankets, resting on a soft pillow with moonlight on my face and sun rays in the morning.

"Please, make it stop scratching," she whimpered.

Just two more minutes, I thought to myself as my heartbeat climbed. Two more minutes, and you can fall back asleep. I began to count in my head, imagining each number appearing and fading until I reached 112 when her peaceful snores resumed.

I was safe to re-enter dreamland, but my thoughts drifted elsewhere. I thought of my previous roommate, Beth. She had been so quiet and subdued, even after her surgery, that she fell asleep as soon as they shut off the fluorescent lights. She was the perfect roommate compared to some of the poor souls trapped here, and I had hoped she would stay my roommate until the miraculous day I was set free. But nothing ever works out for me in the end, for one terrible night, she woke up in a pool of her own blood, shrieking.

The lights clicked on, and they ran in, trying to shield my vision as they wheeled her away. But I caught a glimpse of her face, pale with death clouding her eyes. I knew right then she wasn't coming back.

Honestly, I would've been more surprised if she had actually recovered—it wasn't natural to take out a woman's womb, and Beth was not the first to have complications.

I didn't think her absence affected me until that night when I stared at the empty place where she once slept, wishing I had a stiff drink. I knew it was the only cure for the dread that had settled in the pit of my stomach, though it was the drink itself that brought me to this horrid place to begin with. Even in this modern day, there was no cure for a drunkard, and a lady drunkard was the worst of its kind.

When Ethel arrived, her eyes were as wide as mine must have been on the first day, dark saucers in a narrow face. Her skin was covered in what I assumed were chicken pox scars, her dishwater-blonde hair wispy and thin. I was glad for the company, even though she didn't talk for three days. Until the night she murmured, "They're scratching—please make them stop."

It unnerved me, but I assumed she was having a bad dream. Nightmares tended to occur in a place devoid of hope. The following day, I opened my eyes to see her pacing, biting her lip behind the veil of her stringy hair.

"What is it?" I asked with a yawn.

"You'll think I'm crazy." Her voice was as tiny as her frame.

"We're in the nuthouse, doll. Having people think you're crazy is something you need to get used to."

She paused, wringing her hands as she stared at me with her big saucer eyes. "Do they really take away your lady parts here?" she whispered.

I sighed. "Sometimes. Sometimes they give you medicine that makes you drool, and sometimes, they make you take baths with ice. Every patient endures one kind of torture or another—the trick is convincing them you need the lesser evil."

She resumed her pace. "Then I definitely don't want to tell them."

"Tell them what?" I asked patiently. We didn't have any windows, but I could tell it was almost morning. The nurses would be in soon, and her instincts were right—if they caught her manically pacing, she could easily be on her way to surgery the next week.

"It feels like something is burrowing in my brain."

"Like an insect?"

"Yes, late at night. I hear the scratches."

"Is that why you're here?"

"No, I'm here because my foster father put me here."

"Ah," I said softly. "My father put me here, too."

From that day forward, she and I were friends. She never told me her exact diagnosis, and I did look for any telltale signs when she spoke, but other than the scratching, there was nothing wrong with her. She laughed when things were funny, cried when we talked about freedom and grew cold and hard when it was time for therapy. They put her on the ice baths and drool cocktails, but we both tongued our meds to take at night so we could sleep through the cries that echoed through the halls. But even the meds didn't stop her dream self from telling me about the scratches, and they never stopped me from waking up to hear it.

One evening, she came to our room in tears, babbling that her foster father had come to visit and told the doctors how he found her as a young child. That she'd lived in a filthy, bug-infested house, and doctors had to pull out the insects that had gotten stuck in her ears. That even though they successfully removed them, and she was given a good family and a good home, she still heard them scratching. The shrinks pressed her until she admitted she lied about them ever going away; she heard them still each time she slept.

"It's not all in my mind, Laura," she told me between sobs. "They still get in there, I swear."

I tried to soothe her, though I've never been good at that sort of thing. "Don't you think the doctors can see inside your ears?" I asked her gently. "If you had bugs in there, they would know."

Her expression darkened. "Don't tell me you don't believe me either."

"Please don't be upset with me—" I tried, but she flopped onto her bed with her back to me. I sighed, pulling a drool pill out of the tiny hole in my mattress and rolling over to get some sleep.

My eyes did not open until the morning. The room was quiet; her back still turned to me. I yawned, surprised I'd slept through the night. Maybe the pills they were giving me were getting stronger.

I threw off my blanket to stretch my legs. "You still mad at me?" I asked her.

She offered no response. I put on my plain cotton robe—the one that was so thin it was pointless—and went over to her bedside. "I do believe you," I began, but as I cupped her shoulder, I realized she was ice cold. I recoiled, instinctively pulling my hand back, but her body rolled over, revealing a gruesome purple mask where her face had been.

I started to shake, not wanting to fixate on the tiny bugs that crawled out her ears and through the delicate skin of her eyelids, scuttling along her poor pock-marked skin before retreating into a mouth where death had frozen an eternal scream.

I can't remember what happened after that, but my consciousness returned to see a circle of nurses surrounding me, staring worriedly as I fought the straps they'd used to tie me to the bed. "There were bugs inside her!" I screamed. "She tried to tell me there were bugs! I saw them crawling out of her ears!"

The kindest nurse among them looked at me with a sad smile. "Laura, it's impossible for bugs to burrow into a person's ear. They get trapped sometimes, but they are easily removed. Ethel was a very disturbed girl."

"I saw them! I fucking saw them!" I shrieked, even though I knew I was going to regret it. I couldn't help it. I was hysterical. "You people are fucking monsters —you should have listened to her!"

"Enough of that language, young lady," the nurse snapped. "Jane, please give her 50 milligrams. Dr. Floyd wants to see her."

I thrashed as the needle slid into my arm, fighting the inevitable. I would be unconscious soon, and I knew what would happen while I was out. I let escape one final defiant cry before I submitted to the rush of oblivion slithering through my veins. One last breath and I was plunged into darkness.

I felt better the next morning. They'd moved me to a new, single room, and the bed was a lot softer than my old one. I knew I was on a lot of drugs, but I didn't mind. I didn't even mind when I lifted the blankets to see the bandages wrapped around my abdomen, nor the crimson roses seeping to the surface.

I didn't have to leave the room at all, the nurses wearing big smiles as they brought me soup and medication. Maybe things will get better for me, I thought. Maybe they'd even let me out soon.

In fact, I was thoroughly convinced that maybe I was wrong this whole time—maybe I was just hysterical, and they really did fix me. I knew there was no way bugs could survive in a person's brain for years, and there was no way I saw them coming out of Ethel in death.

But as I closed my eyes and drifted into dreamland, I heard the faintest of sounds in my ears.

It sounded as if something was inside them, scratching.

DAUGHTER.

SHE KEPT our baby teeth in a jar next to her bedside. We never questioned it until we were older, when our cherubic peers laughed after discovering we'd never heard of the Tooth Fairy. Mother hadn't prepared us like she had for Santa Claus: "There is no such thing! I buy all your gifts because I love you. Let the other kids believe that nonsense. Not my girls."

I briefly wondered, as I sat despondently on the plastic chair in her room, who would get the teeth when she died.

"Mom, we brought you flowers." My middle sister had the type of voice that sounded as if she'd unravel at any moment. It chimed along with the heart monitor beeps and breathing tube gasps dueling for Loudest Machine at Mother's Bedside.

I looked at hands kneading themselves on my lap, hoping no one would notice the red sores along my nail beds. Since her stroke, I'd started chewing my cuticles again.

My brother-in-law gazed out the window, bored, while my sister continued her one-sided conversation with the shriveled husk covered in hospital sheets. She spoke too loudly, reminiscent of when painfully white Americans try to communicate with non-English speakers.

"I need a cigarette," I announced.

Neither of them looked in my direction.

Bitter wind smacked my face as I fled the stale building, trying to shake off the dismal energy I'd absorbed with each step down the courtyard corridor.

"Doesn't Donna look like the Crypt Keeper?"

I looked up to see my youngest sister standing under a 'No Smoking' sign, pulling from a Marlboro Light.

"Matches her soul," I replied, not missing a beat. I fished around in my pockets for my vape, awkwardly brandishing the bulky, purple apparatus.

"Constance Adams vapes now?" my sister snorted. The wind tossed around her bleached blonde waves. "Now I've seen everything."

"I quit when I had Ben."

"Another reason why one should not have children."

It was hard to determine what was more embarrassing—the obnoxious vape itself or the giant bubblegum-scented clouds it created. Regardless, the nicotine soon worked its magic on my nerves, allowing passage to the waves of jealousy I always felt near Celeste. Not only was she the most attractive sibling, but she'd broken away as soon as she turned eighteen, married well, embarked on a successful career, and, most importantly, had no children. "I refuse to get pregnant," she once told me. "I'm not going to risk turning into her."

I looked back at the hospice wing of Loving Care

Nursing Home, thinking of my own children. I'd taken great pains to ensure I'd never be her, and yet, the fear remained.

"I'm not going back in there." Celeste extinguished her cigarette on the signpost.

I couldn't blame her. The last time I'd been in a care home was at the age of eight when Donna dragged me along to visit my grandmother. I could still recall the click of heels as the nuns marched down a hallway soured by the reek of unkempt bedpans.

"I'll call you later."

We both knew she wouldn't.

I eventually headed back to my car without telling anyone goodbye, trying to push out the waves of memories that always seemed to hit when we saw each other. Visions of three blonde girls skipping joyfully in our backyard, safe and warm under the veil of delusion. Blissfully unaware that their bouncing locks were routinely threaded into their mother's quilt. Because she wanted to keep them close to her.

I slammed the car door and shakily turned the ignition. Abrasive guitar filled the van as the radio flipped on, but it wasn't loud enough to push out the memory of her gripping fistfuls of my hair—recently dyed red—while she chopped and sobbed that I'd ruined my natural beauty. The same sob that came out of her when she grabbed my freshly sliced-up legs after discovering I'd become a cutter. "I did not take any medication when I had you because I wanted to feel the pain of your birth! I wanted to feel myself bring you into this world—it was my sacrifice! And this is how you repay me? This is what you do to the precious body I created?"

I stopped at the gas station on the way home and bought a pack of cigarettes.

———

I stared at my eighteen-year-old visage eternally trapped in a frame on my mother's wall. Like a shrine of children, four portraits of forced smiles and dead eyes hung in a perfect line above four corresponding Precious Moments figurines. Mine held a paint palette and brush.

Celeste's voice drifted from the other room. "Carric, you're being ridiculous. Hire a fucking attorney and be done with it."

"Where did Constance go? She's the oldest—she should be doing it."

I sighed, entering my mother's living room to see my sisters squared up, ready to pounce. "I'll take care of it."

They both blinked.

"You will?" Carrie's eyes welled with tears of relief.

"Yeah. I'll call tomorrow," I promised.

Celeste curtly bobbed her head and swept out of the room, leaving a lingering trail of Victoria's Secret perfume and cigarettes.

Carrie nervously backed toward the door. "Matt is waiting for me in the car."

"You're dismissed," I said, attempting to be playful.

She scurried off, and as her Chrysler rolled down the driveway of our childhood home, I took a deep breath and surveyed the living room. The thin layer of dust that had settled in Donna's absence didn't do much to distract from its sterility. This house had been meticulously polished for over twenty years.

I moved to the piano and lightly traced the long untouched keys. Piano lessons I never finished were only one of the dozens of activities my mother pushed me through. Donna's daughter played basketball, baseball, volleyball, and soccer; she acted, modeled, joined the swim team, became a cheerleader, sang, played the clarinet, painted... All so she could beam with pride, bathing in the attention. It only stopped when I rebelled, and she found her new obsession: "It's time to take your pills, Constance."

Above the piano hung a solitary portrait. A beaming young man with bright eyes and a full smile surrounded by dozens of smaller photos boasting his achievements. He wore the same toothy grin, only at different ages, as he donned his Mom-inspired costumes: basketball star, chess player, valedictorian. This was her true shrine, the shrine of my younger brother, Matt. She'd finally gotten her perfect child fifteen years after the disappointment that was Celeste.

"Your reply to her was the most childish thing I've ever read," was the last thing Matt ever said to me. It was at our father's funeral service, years after the conversation in question, when I finally removed her access to my kids. After five-year-old Ben told me between sobs that there was no such thing as Santa, and if I let him live with Grammy, she'd buy him everything he ever wanted.

I ignored him, grateful to watch the extended family finally witness her complete apathy for our father as she filled every conversation with talk of Matt's accomplishments and how he'd soon be studying abroad. I didn't cry during the service. I was glad at least someone broke free.

The balcony loomed over me as I went to the kitchen to get a cup of water. I'm not sure why I by-passed the glassware cabinet for the smaller one above the sink, but I pulled it open without hesitation. I paused when I realized the pill bottles were gone, longing to gaze upon the sea of white and orange, neatly-stacked plastic containers. I licked my lips as the euphoric recall hit, and soon the chalky memory of crushed pills pulled saliva into my mouth.

I slammed the cabinet shut and turned on the faucet, taking a few deep breaths as the sound of running water calmed me. It'd been over a decade since I touched a drink or pill after years of taking psychiatric medicine I didn't need. I'd refused to be Donna's golden child, so she decided I would be her lost cause. A sad story to tell at family gatherings. So she could cry and be soothed.

I swallowed a few gulps of water before my phone buzzed.

"Are you coming home?" My husband's worried voice came through the speaker. "Do you need me to pick you up?"

"Are the kids good?" I asked.

"Yeah, I just got them some McDonald's."

"Thank you so much for taking care of them. I'll be home soon."

I took another swig of water and reminded myself why I was there. I pulled open the silverware drawer to find the set of keys pushed to the back, irritated that my hands were still shaking.

The tarnished metal keys rattled as I ascended the stairs, and I tried to calm my nausea. With no one to clean the house or maintain her dozens of air fresheners, the sickly smell had pushed its way through.

Before Matt disappeared, Donna insisted he sleep in the bedroom next to hers. As I passed her nauseatingly pink room, I half-expected her to emerge in that awful nightgown she refused to throw away.

"If you leave me to rot in a place like this," she once hissed to eight-year-old me, "I will haunt you for the rest of your days." Her eyes were black, only shifting to offer the nursing home nuns a saccharine smile as they walked past.

"Then why did you put Grandma here?" I asked her innocently.

"Grandma never loved me," she shot back. "I love you girls—I do everything for you."

I reached my brother's room and hurried to fit the key into the lock. The door stuck, and when I finally managed to wedge it open, I was met with a thick swarm of flies. Swatting them away as I held back vomit, I raced to open the window. I lingered there, watching the sunset beyond the expanse of perfect houses with perfectly manicured lawns.

"Mom is going to die soon," I said.

The wax figure of my brother did not respond.

She'd kept his room exactly how he had left it, complete with a few dirty basketball shorts and shoes strewn across the floor. The curled edges of aging posters lifted in the breeze.

I walked over to remove the tarnished crucifix from his wall. "This can be the first to go," I said.

If Matt was still alive, he'd probably tell me I was being childish. But Matt was not alive.

When I first discovered him, I was pregnant. Although I lived a few blocks down the road, I hadn't visited Donna since Dad's funeral—almost five years. I hadn't planned on it until my husband's family wanted some of my old pictures for the baby shower. I knew she still had the album, and I begrudgingly decided to make the trek. I thought I dodged a bullet when I discovered the front door had been left unlocked, and Donna was nowhere to be found.

Some people feel safe and welcome in their childhood home, but that was never my experience. Still, the energy felt heavier than ever before, and as I gingerly made my way up the stairs, I couldn't understand why her spotless home smelled so awful.

When I opened the door to see him lying there, I froze. But I didn't need to investigate; I knew without a shadow of a doubt that his old baby teeth were placed neatly inside those wax gums. I didn't have to touch the sandy waves to know his real hair had been glued to its wax head.

It did take me several minutes, however, to realize that his actual body lay beneath the wax shell, decomposing organs eating their way through the mattress and leaving a sticky black puddle on the floor.

"How dare you go into your brother's room!"

I hadn't heard her come home. Startled, I fell forward, smacking my hip on the dresser. "Is that—is that really him?"

Donna had grown even more revolting with time, her beady eyes bulging from a pale, swollen face. "He overdosed on drugs," she wailed, "like you did when you were younger. I didn't want anyone to know, so I let you all believe he was missing."

My knees threatened to give way, bile in the back of my throat. Her alcohol-laced breath served as a welcome reprieve from the suffocating stench of the room.

She grabbed a nearby can of air freshener, releasing peony mist over the bloated, rotting remains of my little brother. "He'll be fine, right here where I can take care of him. I took care of your grandmother, too, remember?"

"You put Grandma in a nursing home."

She dropped her hysterics. "Your grandmother was a horrible woman." She sniffed, indignant. "You girls don't know how badly she treated me. I mixed up all her pills as a courtesy. She would've lived a horrible last few years."

I would tell my husband months later that people always reveal their true selves. You just have to listen to their words. For in that moment, I understood everything.

"I didn't want him to leave," she finally admitted as she resumed her tears, letting them pour down her face as she approached the bedside to stroke the wax lump's hair.

"I-I need a cigarette," I managed to croak out, stumbling from the room.

Miraculously, she did not follow.

I went to the emergency room that night for a miscarriage. The attending knew my mother from nursing school and gushed over how much I looked like her.

As soon as I got home, blood still seeping from between my legs, I locked myself in the bathroom. I dry-shaved my head with an old razor, admiring the streams of red dripping in pretty lines down my forehead.

My husband stopped me before I took the razor to my face.

The memory faded as I left Matt's bedroom and entered hers.

An old Bible lay on her bedside table, next to the jar of our baby teeth and her pill case. I recalled worrying that the EMTs would check it when they arrived on the scene, but there seemed to be no cause for alarm. Older women with health issues and drinking habits tended to have strokes. More surprising was they didn't even question the odor coming from the other room.

I picked up the plastic case and sprinkled the pills out on her bed, admiring the mosaic it created. I wondered which of the ones I tampered with were the ones that finally took her down. I guess I inherited her gift.

I grabbed the Bible next, joyfully ripping out the pages and watching them flutter to the ground. *Blasphemy*, she would have chastised if she knew. What a good Catholic her daughter had become.

I opened her dresser drawers, pulling out shirt after shirt, dress after dress, until her room was in disarray. To see the chaos I created soothed me as I poured the gasoline and steadied my fingers as I lit the match.

Flames had devoured most of the house before the authorities showed up. I'd used Donna's voice when I called, mimicking the same hysteric-laced inflection she'd used when she called the psych ward to haul her daughter away. Donna Theatrics, Celeste called it.

I also cried her crocodile tears as they gently questioned me, even hugging the firefighter who retrieved her Precious Moments figurines. I thought of my Ben as I thumbed the ash off the one holding the paint palette and easel. He loved to paint like his mommy; perhaps I could give it to him. I gently wrapped the figurine in my scarf as I turned to walk home. I pushed the horrors of the night away, thinking only of my sweet, blonde-haired boy. My precious, perfect son.

Maybe tomorrow would be the day I'd throw his jar of baby teeth away. The one I kept by my bedside.

LAURA WAS TIRED.

Tired of the long hours, the walks on eggshells, the black eyes. Tired of forcing her lips into a passable smile with each lie. Tired of the way the snooty women at the grocery store looked at her, with that curious mix of knowing and pity in their judgmental eyes. But mostly, she was tired of watching her own blood spiral down the shower as she hugged her knees and cried over the latest fall-down-the-stairs-ran-into-a-door-insert-bullshit-excuse-here. If it wasn't for Johnny, she would leave.

An overgrown cherub with freckles and a gap-tooth grin, her son managed to pull her through each day. It was no secret he was a brilliant child—perhaps too bright for his own good—and her heart burst with pride each time he came home with another perfect grade. You could barely see any gold on the old Frigidaire, but she hung up every paper as if it was the very first time. Deep down, she knew if she could just survive until he was older, he'd take the world by storm. If only he'd give up his obsession with the crows.

"Mama, we need to put out food for Samuel!"

Laura shuddered. She hated Samuel, a big ol' bastard with a crooked beak and an awkward tuft of feathers sticking out from its side like he'd once fought a battle he'd barely won. "I know, baby." She sighed as his skinny frame appeared in the doorway. She'd pulled up her stockings just in time, the opaque tan obscuring her latest crop of bruises. "We have ten minutes to get to Mrs. Meyer's house, so please hurry."

He darted off, and she tucked her blouse into her skirt with another sigh. She was grateful Johnny was older at least; when he was younger, she would have to stop everything to gather peanuts, popcorn, or whatever she imagined crows eat, and leave them scattered on the front porch, lest she deal with a tantrum that would last the entire length of Berry Street. Now, he gathered it all himself, joyful to see that each evening, the porch was clear.

The day pressed on, as days often do, and when Laura pulled in the station wagon to see Bill's rusty truck in the driveway, her stomach lurched. Her eyes darted to her watch to confirm she was not late; he must not have stopped at the bar after work. That was a very, very bad sign.

She tried not to vomit as shaky legs took her toward the house. The rip in the screen door looked like a sneer as she approached, and before her hand even touched the handle, he was there.

"Why was there good food scattered all over my front porch?"

"Why are you home so early?"

"Answer the question, Laura."

She could smell the gin on him, but she could no

longer tell if it was fresh or from the night before. "It's just scraps, Bill."

"Since when do we have a dog?" His left eye bulged from its socket, the little vein near his temple throbbing.

She licked her dry lips. He was turning. "Mrs. Meyer gives Johnny scraps from her dog's food. For the crows."

"*For the crows*," he mocked. "You and that crazy ol' bitch are ruining that boy. He shouldn't be wasting good food like that." He'd grown close enough that spittle flew from his lips and dusted her cheek. His pupils had grown, eclipsing his eyes. His monster mask.

"Please, Bill, I have to pick up Johnny," she whispered, knowing it was too late. She knew what happened when he put on the mask.

———

Her alarm clock failed the following day, and she slept straight through daybreak. Her head throbbed as she picked it off her gore-crusted pillowcase. She swayed as she found her ratty bathrobe, pulling it around her bruised frame as she dialed the rotary for the diner.

"One more time, Laura and we're gonna have to let you go," her manager said on the other line.

She refused to look in the mirror as she staggered to the bathroom, yesterday's lunch finally coming back up with the old familiar tang of sour metal. She reached up to feel her lip had been split. She held a washcloth under the faucet and pressed it against the wound. Curious why Johnny hadn't woken her up, she went to his bedroom, only to find he'd already left.

The made bed and lack of bookbag let her know he'd made it to Mrs. Meyer's, but had he walked? Had Bill taken him in before work?

Her head hurt too much to speculate, so she shuffled towards the coffee pot. She didn't want to think about what he would say when he learned she missed work. She grabbed the bottle of aspirin from the cabinet and winced as the acidic coffee chaser bit the cut on her lip.

A loud caw cracked through the air. She jumped, turning to see the grotesquely large Samuel filling the window as he swooped onto the porch. She blinked, thoroughly confused. Had Johnny been able to feed the crow in front of his father? The morning was becoming stranger and stranger. She set down her cup of coffee, determined to see for herself.

As she searched for her slippers, the sound of cawing intensified as if hundreds of birds had joined him, squawking and fluttering on the porch. Unable to find her slippers, she pulled on a pair of Bill's old boots, stumbling as she pushed open the door. The sunlight pierced her eyes for a moment, the screen door clanging shut as she made her way to the front of the house.

She rounded the corner and nearly slipped, but she caught herself just in time.

No one really prepares you for shock, but she had seen it in the movies and was certain she felt it now. For her hair did not stand on end, nor did she scream, nor did she faint like the women on TV. Instead, she peered calmly at her son, standing amidst dozens of crows, laughing and dancing like he did as a little boy. They danced with them, swooping and diving as they took turns happily devouring their latest meal.

She didn't even shiver when she saw Samuel perched on what was left of Bill's face, his broken body splayed out on the front steps. She didn't even flinch as he pulled an eyeball from its socket, slurping it down before giving her a loud, satisfied squawk.

Johnny noticed her staring and stopped spinning. "You can go get ready, Mama," he called to her with a smile and a wave. "I already fed Samuel."

RIPPER.

IT IS important that you know it was not me.

According to groups of well-learned, scholarly types, it is not possible for a woman to have the level of depravity required for purposeful murder—it is strictly a male-dominated realm. Those who have risen to that level of infamy—the Lizzie Bordens, the Delphine LaLauries, the Elizabeth Bathorys—have been properly detested and considered anomalies. People speak of them with shock, horror, and awe, for how could a woman, a creature biologically intended to love and nurture, be able to commit such vile atrocities? Women are simply too fragile, too *hysterical* for murder. Murder is grisly, messy—and what woman would want blood stains on her dress?

It is for all of these reasons, and a great many more, that it simply was not me.

I will not deny, however, that the thoughts are there. Perhaps if I had been born into a poor family, it wouldn't have been so easy. Or if my outer shell was more plain and I wasn't able to attract so much attention. One could speculate endlessly, I suppose, but for whatever the reason, I cannot sit idly amongst an array of boring people, chattering on about the weather or the dreadful state of the nation, and not imagine their deaths. While other women may be content working on their cross-stitching or writing letters, I am content when I imagine the kindly young suitor come to call with a letter opener in his heart.

But this does not mean I am capable of murder. I have an overactive mind, the tragic result of educating a woman, what happens when her corset is a bit too tight, or when she does not properly learn and recite her scripture.

Had my sister lived past the age of eight, she would have been a proper lady, someone to distract them from me. I did miss her when she died, but she had found my stash of cat eyes buried in the garden, along with a few of their corpses where she intended to plant daisies. She needed to be disposed of, and besides, I wanted her collection of dolls.

But allow me to remind you that I am a woman, and therefore not capable of murder, especially not as a young girl. I did not have the fortitude, the required strength, to pry her eyes out of her sockets while she lay dead in her coffin before the family buried her in the plot not far from our home. Furthermore, young girls do not have the mental capacity to realize that keeping eyeballs and tongues in jars for extended periods of time is far more trouble than it's worth and that collecting teeth is far more satisfactory an endeavor. Dentistry is a male occupation—men enjoy the satisfying crack made when one pulls a tooth out of its jawbone with a set of pliers, certainly not a young woman preparing for marriage. They do not have the time, nor the stomach, to peruse anatomical texts and memorize all the parts of the body. They cannot possibly saw through bones to remove appendages or break open chest plates to pull out hearts.

I digress.

My purpose in writing this letter is to maintain my innocence, to explain how it is simply impossible for me to have dissected every corpse found in my backyard. My husband, my poor, willfully blind husband, graciously took the blame and was promptly hung. I miss him too, come to think of it, but I am certain after some time he would have found the handmade dolls in my attic with their human hair wigs or even the living dolls I keep in the shed, whose mouths and eyes are sewn shut so they cannot scream nor find their way out. Which reminds me, I will be needing a new collection soon—as they expire, they let out a dreadful stench that attracts far more insects than I feel comfortable with.

Sometimes I wonder what my life would have been like had I birthed children. They are what keep a woman sane, give her a purpose in life. Perhaps if I had been able to provide my poor husband with an heir, things would have been different. They certainly would have given me something to use to maintain my innocence, to prove that I am a good, decent woman and certainly not one whose house swallowed five different servants over the last six months, even after my murderous husband had been hanged.

But, childless or not, there is still no possible way I could have managed to gut and dismember all the poor souls whose parts have been used to decorate the manor, no possible way I could have dragged their bodies down to the cellar for the cats, no way on earth I could have stomached the bleaching of their skulls, the jarring of their innards, nor the filing of their bones for furniture. Women don't make furniture.

And I am a woman, after all.

SOULMATES.

THE LONG AUGUST drought finally yielded to a gentle rainfall, though the clouds were unable to completely hide the moon, which peeked out enough to cast a sliver of light across her face. It brought a crispness to the air, and she burrowed under an extra blanket as she stared out into the night.

She found herself in a restless half-sleep as if the distant rolling thunder brought something with it, and when her eyes opened to deliver her from her dreams, she saw him sitting next to her on the bed, gazing out her window.

"I was having the most wonderful dream," she murmured to his profile. "Is it time?"

"Yeah," he sighed. "No wonder you live here. It's beautiful."

She sat up, stretching the sleep out of her shoulders and the cobwebs out of her eyes before giving her husband a light kiss goodbye. She didn't bother to get dressed, slipping on the robe that matched her black lace nightgown. She drifted to each bedroom in her house, kissing her slumbering children before joining him on the porch. "I'm ready," she told him.

By the time they arrived at their destination, the sun had risen, though it was cooled by a veil of cloud. Fog blanketed the desolate seaside town, swirling around the abandoned lighthouse as they drew closer.

"It's beautiful," she remarked.

He offered his hand as they maneuvered around the stones and broken pieces of building that scattered the grass leading up to the door. When he pushed it open, they were hit by the musky scent of age and moisture-rich decay, a flutter of bats escaping out of sight. As dilapidated as the lighthouse looked from afar, the inside was warm, cozy even, the broken windows letting in the crash of waves and the brackish sea air.

Neither one of them spoke, curling up in each other's limbs on a bed that creaked when they moved.

"Are you sure you want this?" she whispered, her breath tickling his ear.

"I've brought death to so many," he sighed.

"You've freed many from their suffering," she corrected, swirling her fingers through his hair. They traced the bridge of his nose and the curve of his lips, down the slope of his neck to the jagged scars that covered his arms. She spent time there, listening to their tragic stories with her fingertips.

"Let's wait until nightfall," he told her.

They walked the shoreline, footprints in the sand as she collected sea glass, filling the mason jars left behind with shades of green, red, and blue. When the sun set, it finally pushed copper through the fog, filling up the room and rusting his messy locks as he lay back down on the bed. He crossed his fingers on his chest, staring out at the sea.

She stared down at him. "Now?"

"I'm ready," he replied.

She took him into her lap, cradling him for a moment to her chest, trying not to let the sorrow creep in. "Are you sure you want this?" she repeated.

He reached up to stroke her face, a sad smile on his. "I'm going to do this with or without you, love. Much rather it be with you."

A flock of seagulls called out overhead, and their eyes met, holding each other's gaze as she pressed the glass into the delicate skin of his neck, right under his ear, making sure to press into the jugular as she slid it all the way to his other. She let the glass fall away, holding his hands as blood gashed from the violent opening, fighting tears as she watched the life fade from his eyes.

She held him until he was no longer warm, and it was just her, the night, and a corpse, the entire bed coated in sticky crimson. She withdrew, draping his body with one of the blankets, shaking out the mason jars to leave a mosaic of sea glass surrounding him.

The night air was much cooler than the daylight, though still heavy with moisture, making gooseflesh of her skin. She listened to the calming waves as they caressed her feet, washing the blood away.

NIGHTMARES.

LARRY WAS EXHAUSTED, the sort of run-over-by-a-car exhausted one feels after a three-day bender. His hands shook as he tried to lift the styrofoam cup to his lips, black spots in the corners of his vision. One more day, he thought to himself. One more day and this whole mess would be over.

He wasn't a terrible person. He was just a junkie, the worst kind, who makes insane promises to whoever is proposing *the stupid thing* so he can get his next fix. This time, he hadn't even realized what he was agreeing to until he was in the van, and the two men he was supposed to work with dragged the struggling lump of blankets out of its cozy mansion and into the trunk. The warm placidity of his last hit still lingered in his veins, enough that it soothed over the sound of the child's cries.

It wasn't until they arrived at the old barn and it was his turn to watch over the kid that the reality of Larry's situation hit him.

At first, he tried to comfort the little boy, careful not to reveal too much of his face behind the ski mask, but it was pointless. The kid was terrified. Rightly so, but

Larry figured it could be much worse for the kid—he might be a hopeless drug addict, but at least he wasn't the type to harm kids.

The next day was harder. He had a little bit of his stash left to keep him from getting sick, but it wasn't enough to make him feel *good*. His mind was left free to roam, scolding him for getting involved in some kidnapping scheme, even if that meant a few extra bucks and a nice fat bag to go home with. He tried to focus on how nice it would be to pay the rent for his apartment, maybe even get the hot water turned back on. Skip a visit to the food bank and walk right into the grocery store. Anything to distract from the whimpering lump in the loft above him.

The sun disappeared behind the clouds, and he checked the flip phone the guys had given him. Still nothing. When they dumped the kid and him off at the barn, they told him tonight there would either be someone to relieve him of his shift or someone to grab the kid because the ransom went through. He tried not to play every worst-case scenario in his head. *They'll be here. I just gotta be patient.*

He peered out the broken, dusty window, lifting the sweaty ski mask from his face to suck in the fresh air. There was no one around them for miles, just an endless dark cornfield dancing in the breeze under a blanket of stars. In any other circumstance, Larry would have thought it was beautiful.

The kid let out a loud sob, interrupting his moment of peace. Larry shoved his mask back on and headed up the narrow stairs to the loft. "Knock that off, would ya? You're about to go home soon. Just take a nap or whatever."

The kid didn't respond. He hadn't budged from

where he'd been left in the hay, the snacks Larry had brought him earlier untouched.

Larry frowned. "You should eat, kid."

Again, no response.

Larry sighed and lumbered back down the ladder. *They'd better come through soon.*

The old wooden barn creaked and moaned as it fought the building wind outside. He found a spot in the barn to recline, wondering if he should try to get a few minutes of rest. He hadn't slept since they arrived, but it wasn't as if he couldn't get away with it—the kid hadn't moved a muscle since they brought him here, and if he did get up and try to flee, the sound would surely wake him. Larry was a light sleeper by nature, with or without intoxicants. Sleep pulled at his eyelids, weighing him down with its promise. He decided to fight against it, taking another sip of his cold, black coffee as he looked back at his phone.

A sharp pop above jolted him.

He cursed as the meager light in the barn promptly went out, bathing him in total darkness. Larry cursed; he didn't know a damn thing about breaker boxes or whatever the hell was providing the barn with electricity. He found the flashlight on his phone, dismayed to find out its pathetic blue glow only reached arm's length. He shut it back off, highly annoyed. His eyes would just have to adjust to the darkness.

It occurred to him suddenly that the kid had stopped crying. He would have thought the sudden power outage might have panicked him more. Instead, there was just a low steady creak of floorboards, reminding him of the sound of trees about to fall in the woods. He wondered if it was just the barn itself; over the last few minutes, what was originally a lovely breeze had turned into a whirling storm. But he heard it again. This was different, closer. He fumbled for the pistol they'd given him earlier. The cold metal in his palm woke him up, and he began to creep along the perimeter, making sure no one had snuck in.

As he made his way back, he could have sworn he saw a man standing in the corner, but it wasn't possible for a man to be that thin and that tall. It was a damn hallucination, and he knew it, one that came from lack of sleep and the beginning of withdrawals. It had to be, he decided. But as much as he told himself that the impossibly slender, looming creature nearby was not real, he didn't want to go any closer to find out. Instead, he crept back up the ladder to the loft. "Kid," he whispered. "Hey, kid, are you okay?"

The lump of blankets was still there, but the kid was not moving, nor was he responding. Maybe he'd finally fallen asleep.

Larry heard the creak again, but this time, it sounded more like a groan. He looked back at the impossible thing, grateful to see it had disappeared. This was getting ridiculous, he thought miserably. He was sleep-deprived and fiending. He was going to give it one more hour, and he'd take the damn kid home himself. Shit, maybe his parents would give him a reward for doing the right thing.

He headed back down the ladder, deciding to ignore the groan. He watched a lump of impossibly big spiders make their way across the shadowy wall, too many spiders to count, but he knew damn well that spiders did not travel together in such a solid mass. He was imagining spiders that acted like ants.

He found his spot on the floor and shut his eyes against the nonsense, deciding that sleep would be the best course of action to take. Who knew when the next time would be when he could rest? He'd feel the vibration of the phone on his lap if they decided to come. If he kept himself awake too much longer, he might lose his wits altogether.

"Mister?" The kid's tiny voice scared him half to death.

"Holy shit, kid," he swore, glad to see that the spiders were gone as he hurried back up the rungs. "What do you want?"

The boy's cheeks were streaked with tears, his eyes red, mucus dripping from his nose. His pajamas were ripped and torn, which was a shame because they were the really nice, matching kind that Larry's mother could never afford when he was a kid. "Mister, I'm really sorry, but they came to get me."

Larry frowned, looking down and around the barn. He saw nothing, no headlights in the windows, no arriving people, not even the hallucinations. "Kid, I'm tired," he sighed. "You need to get some sleep."

"That's the thing, I can't sleep without them," the boy told him. "You know how kids usually have bad nightmares? Well, I kinda like mine."

Larry stared at him, wishing like hell he had more drugs.

"My dad was really mad about it at first. They know I need my rest."

"Kid, go to sleep." Annoyed, Larry made his way down the ladder again, but this time, he couldn't reach the ground.

Dozens of limbless bodies slithered on the floor of the barn, torsos with human faces holding rotten eyes and horrible mouths that snapped at his feet. Larry screamed, scrambling back up to the loft as he pulled out his gun. He shook so bad he dropped it, watching the human worms wiggle right over it, trying to jump and clasp their sharp teeth on whatever part of his flesh they could.

"Kid–*kid!*" he screamed, unable to do Paul much else as he backed into the poor child in his scramble, pressing him against the wall.

"Oh, hiya, Mister."

Larry jumped to see he hadn't pushed a young kid but a bulbous clown, its stomach bursting out of suspenders as red as its nose. The perversion of hilarity grinned at him beneath hollowed-out eyes, its jaw coming unhinged like a snake. The kid stood next to it, wearing a sad smile as he held its hand.

"I'm sorry, Mister, they know I'm tired," he said with a yawn.

Larry shrieked then, one of those high-pitched sounds you hear in movies that you don't think you're capable of. Then he lost control of his legs, tumbling from the loft in a bundle of frantic limbs. He wasn't sure when he finally wet himself, but a part of him was glad the clown didn't have a chance to lick him with its big purple tongue as he fell into the writhing mass on the ground. He thought of his mother then, and how much he wished he could tell her he was sorry, as his nose filled with the stench of rotting meat and the human worms began to feast.

I REMEMBER the first time I saw Will's special drawer.

It was midsummer, so we rarely went into the attic that we'd turned into our own playroom until night, when a cool enough breeze came in through the tiny window that it didn't feel like you were suffocating. But Will was at one of his doctor appointments, and I needed some blank pieces of paper to write on, so up I went into the heat.

The scent of mothballs hit as I climbed the narrow stairs, strengthened by the humidity. I located his pad of drawing paper easily; it was right on his desk near the old dresser, but I paused when I noticed the bottom drawer was open just a tiny crack.

I'd seen his drawings hundreds of times and pretended to love them, just as I pretended to admire any amputee he excitedly pointed out as we walked down the street. But there was something more unnerving about the drawer full of Barbie torsos, something about their mindless, painted smiles that rose above Will's sketches of naked, limbless beauties with haunting eyes. I imagined him sitting up there, lovingly removing their limbs like the wings off a butter-fly, discarding them in the trash, and setting the torsos on the blanket lining his drawer.

I slammed it shut, swallowing hard as I grabbed the sketch pad and hurried back down the stairs.

Will was a fantastic artist, something I hadn't inherited, and there was something magical about watching him bring his creations to life in pencil. But I think I encouraged him to draw mainly to give him a reason to keep both his arms.

"I can always teach myself to draw with my left hand," he pointed out. "I don't need both."

"You need one hand to draw and one to hold down the paper," I argued. "Don't hurt your arms, Will."

I'd like to think I had an influence on him, but a part of me wondered if he was just pacifying me until he could finish the job he'd started on his legs. As if they were the true villains in his wonderfully artistic but broken mind.

"It's an extremely rare mental disorder," they explained to my hysterical mother the night it happened. Who *they* were specifically, I can't remember; all adults seem the same when you're a child. All I can recall were their shiny shoes on the linoleum floors, picking up the fluorescent lights overhead.

"It's a problem with your brother's brain," a woman clarified for my child's ears. She was wearing a white coat and glasses, and when she peered over them, I noticed her eyes were the color of chocolate milk. "We just have to ensure you don't have the same kind of brain since he's your twin."

Much later, my older sister, Sarah, explained what I saw, the thing that no one else in my family ever wanted to mention again. I had no recollection of the incident at the time, but I'd pieced together enough to know I had walked in on my brother in the garage, and whatever I saw was so traumatizing that I blocked out the entire memory. My dreams, however, barely floated by without some flash of nightmarish crimson.

Sarah eventually ran away from home at the age of seventeen. I overheard the neighbor lady commenting that she was just like her mother, running away with a smooth-talking older man who would do nothing but leave her with a child and break her heart. No one could really blame her. It was hard to live with Will and I.

My mother didn't do much to stop Sarah, but by then, her own vices had long become stronger than any inkling of maternal instinct. Come to think of it, I can't recall a time when Mom's breath wasn't sharpened by whiskey, her half-empty Jack bottles stashed all over the house. We would find them in the most random places, even in the attic. Sometimes I wonder if she ever had enough liquid courage to take a peek, and if so, did she ever get close to throwing out the mutilated Barbie dolls. If she had, she never said a word, and we all continued to pretend like we believed Will was just going up there to draw normal things, like a normal kid.

"They hurt, Mike," he whispered the night we decided to camp in the attic. Mom was at the bar, which means she was out for the night, and we lugged our sleeping bags up the stairs to eat stale popcorn and tell each other ghost stories. Mine were always better than his, it was the one thing I was good at, and we'd laid around afterward in dark silence with our flashlights, hoping the ghosts I invented would show up in the spider-webbed crevices of the room.

"They don't really hurt, Will. That's just the part of your brain that's broken," I told him as I created an infinity swirl with my flashlight on the ceiling.

"You know they hurt me," he said. "The doctors just have you afraid to admit it."

It was on our eighteenth birthday when I finally remembered the incident. Mom forgot our birthday every year, and we'd stopped reminding her, instead waiting until she passed out, stealing a couple of her beers and a few cigarettes, and heading out to the garage to light off some celebratory fireworks. This year was just like the others, but Will was quieter than usual, barely cheering when I set one off so loud it made the neighbor's cat squeal. He sipped his beer, ignoring his smoldering cigarette as he stared off into space.

"What is it?" I sighed.

"You know what it is."

I shook my head. "You can't ask me to do it."

"You have to finish it, Mike," he said. "You have to do it, not me. It makes me faint."

I remember staring at him for a long time, seeing the sadness in his eyes. And then it all came rushing back—the two of us in the garage, covered in Will's blood and Sarah's hysterical screams.

I'm not sure how regular siblings love each other. I never really cared much for Sarah, but your twin, it... it's just different. We are connected beyond just the mirror image that people see. I loved my twin enough to give him what he'd always wanted, just like he loved me enough to tell the doctors, who suspiciously looked between us, that he was the one who did it— just like he had back when we were kids.

It's the reason I drove home and cleaned up the

gore-splattered garage and hacksaw before anyone came to investigate and why he sat patiently in the psych ward, accepting their bullshit therapy and the medication that wouldn't help. It's why I would build a ramp up the stairs for his wheelchair and why he would continue to live with me even after Mom finally moved out.

It's how I know that when the time comes when he begs me to take off his arms, I will do it, even if it means I will no longer get to see his beautiful drawings.

I can't explain the depth of our connection. I just know it goes beyond his broken mind.

SLUGGER.

THE BASEBALL BAT fell from my hand and landed on the bathroom floor with a loud crack. The dull fluorescent light in the ceiling flickered on as it always did a few moments after you flipped the switch, revealing my face in the cracked and dingy mirror. The faintest glimpse of a cockroach scurrying across the peeling wallpaper caught my eye but failed to produce a shudder. I was consumed by my reflection, focusing on the line of my jaw, which had already begun to swell beneath a greenish-yellow bruise. My fingers moved across the tender flesh as I wondered how I still managed to keep teeth in my jawbone. A few cuts scratched my face, beads of sweat dotting my forehead. My lips were dry and cracked, my pupils wide within bloodshot eyes.

My mother was dead. I knew this because as my father crumbled from the blow of the bat she bought me for coach pitch three springs ago, I had run to her in search of a steady pulse. When there was none to be found, I didn't waver, for I had grown more than accustomed to the image of my beaten mother sprawled out on the living room floor and my father immobilized next to her in a drunken stupor. I was more surprised by the fact that she had held on so tightly to life over the years, no matter how vicious the attack or how effective his weapon of choice was. I lovingly tucked a lock of hair behind her ear, which left a thin line of red behind her ashen face. "He found us again, huh?" I asked out loud. Sorrow tried to penetrate my hardened heart but to no avail. A tempestuous storm had risen in me, quickening my pulse and blackening my eyes.

After bending down to retrieve the fallen bat, I left the bathroom. My father still lay on the floor, gasping frantic breaths through crack-destroyed lungs, his mouth slackened into a hideous O. A dark shadow of beard covered his skeletal face, eye sockets protruding through stretched, sallow skin that looked like parchment paper. I felt nothing for the thing that lay before me, a man that prison or rehab couldn't fix. A deep and twisted mental disturbance had grown inside him and spilled freely onto anyone who got caught in the storm, his sadism knowing no bounds.

I closed my eyes and envisioned a father I had never met before, a man with dancing blue eyes that matched my own and a smile bursting with kindness and warmth. I imagined him crouching at the pitcher's mound, smacking a baseball into a gloved hand a few times.

"Alright, Anna, hit me a home run!" he called.

The sun hung high and brilliant in the cloudless sky, the warm summer air batting at the ponytail held in place by my baseball cap. I waited for him to pitch it to me and swung, hitting the ball with a deafening crack.

"Way to go, slugger," my dad cheered, scooping up

another ball from the ones collected at his feet. "Ready for another?"

"I'm ready!" I called back.

Chirping birds scattered as I connected with the ball a second time, causing it to sail into the woods behind us. My dad erupted into cheers once more, his voice encouraging me to hit harder and harder. We continued well into the afternoon, me never missing a pitch, until our faces hurt from smiling, and our voices were raw from laughter.

We were down to one more ball before we'd have to go for the scavenger hunt around the park and baseball field to retrieve them all when he paused and straightened. His face had grown serious. "Anna, before this next one, I want to tell you something."

The sky had grown dark, ominous thunder rolling in this distance. The air turned cold, lifting the hairs on the back of my neck. I shivered, staring at the man before me, looking back with earnest eyes. "I just want to say how proud I am of you," he said softly. "You're the best daughter a father could ask for."

"Thank you, Daddy," I replied, the bat suddenly feeling so heavy in my arms. I whispered, "Can I stop now?"

Flashes of the blood-soaked apartment seemed to rip through the fabric of my fantasy, threatening to take him from me. I wished with all that was in me that he could stay. "I'm so tired," I said.

"You can do this," he said firmly. "One more time, and then it's done, for good."

I swallowed the threatening sob of hysteria, gathering my strength. I gripped the bat as hard as I could muster, my knuckles whitening with the strain, finding my footing and steadying my stance.

"I love you, Anna," he said, whipping the ball at me once more.

I swung; the sound of the last hit was so loud, I nearly mistook it for thunder.

My mother's body appeared in the distance, and I was in the apartment again. I moved towards her and gingerly wrapped her fingers around the splintered, maroon-stained bat.

My father's body had completely disappeared, a broken carcass of gore and shattered bones now in its wake. I stepped over it and went into the kitchen. I grabbed the phone to call 911, tasting sour metal as his blood ran from my hair into my mouth. I'd have to wash my face before they arrived. "Yes, 743 Torrance Circle." My voice was calm, as it was every time I had to make the call. "Yes, it's my mom and dad again. No...no, I think they're both dead this time. Okay. Thank you."

I replaced the receiver and waited for the police to come.

SHE'D FORGOTTEN HER KNIFE.

It wasn't that big a deal; it was more of a precaution, really, ever since she saw the story of a masked hiker who attacked a female runner in the woods. She almost threw her phone down in fury—the woods were supposed to be a safe place, especially for those who found solace in its winding paths and acres of green. Was there nowhere a woman could feel safe?

Her husband had gently reminded her that the woods have been a scary place since the dawn of time and suggested she carry a can of mace on her runs. She considered it for a moment but couldn't imagine carrying some bulky container as she pounded the rocky paths, only to struggle with its operation when said attacker decided to make his move. So, she settled on a knife. She bought one at a nearby truck stop, of all places, with a little clip so she could secure it alongside her waist. A pointless precaution, probably, but the sense of badass-ery it gave her as she ran could not be denied.

Today, however, she'd left it behind, but she decided not to be concerned. The trails were empty as the pre-vernal clouds dropped their cold rain onto the earth, scaring away those "nature-lovers" who disliked slippery mud and quickly drenched hair. She was alone as she wound up and down the path by the creek, watching it rush and roar around its rocks, like bodies of water do when reunited with their brethren, birthed by the clouds above.

She ran until her lungs squeezed, and she struggled to scoop in more restorative air, refusing to allow the pain to slow her down. She relished in the hammer of her heart, the ache screaming in her leg muscles.

And then, she saw it, its discovery the thing that finally tempered her swift pace.

She attempted to catch her breath, trying to steady her vision so she could see through its tremor and the insistent raindrops. The longer she stared, the more she was convinced her mind was playing tricks on her, for there was no logical way that a man could be sitting so still on a rock in the middle of a rushing creek. It had to be some formation, a strangely angled tree, or a cluster of garbage settled in just the right way.

Except she was pretty damned sure it had eyes.

She gave up the fight to calm down, her runner's adrenaline quickly replaced by fear. She cursed herself for not bringing her knife, caught halfway between wanting to run back home or creeping closer for a better look. Curiosity was the victor, taking over her legs as they pushed her closer to the lump of unknown amidst the waves.

It grew clearer—a motionless man staring at her from where he sat with bulging eyes in the middle of the creek. He was shirtless, water pouring down purplish skin that appeared as if it had been forcibly stretched over an unnaturally bulbous form. Her rational mind and vision began its own argument, for there was no possible way that such a grotesquely shaped, shirtless man was sitting in the middle of the creek staring at her. Perhaps she was hallucinating, perhaps she'd actually fainted somewhere along her trek, and this was all some wily trick of the unconscious.

Her legs shook as she grew closer.

He didn't blink as she continued to stare at him, his mouth hanging open slackly as if frozen in place, water pooling at his folded legs. Frog was the perfect descriptor, she realized, as she observed his bald head and strange black eyes. The blob that sat before her looked like a giant, hideous frog.

The sensation to flee was finally growing stronger than her curiosity as she looked around, remembering how deep she was in the woods and how she was very much alone. She was slowly backing away when she heard ita low, rumbling croak, like the chorus of a hundred frogs, coming from the direction of the man.

And then she saw the pile of black clothing collected near the edge of the creek, an average-sized shirt laid flat on the rocks. She saw his skin ripple and move as if filled with dozens of tiny creatures, the movement upsetting the stillness of his eyes, now rolling in opposite directions.

What she didn't see as she raced as fast as her legs had ever taken her back to her car near the start of the trail, was the tiny greenish-brown frog that hopped out of his open mouth, and its sibling, who found its way out through the torn flap of skin at his belly, as if displeased at the overcrowding of their new home.

BITE.

"IT'S HARD TO SAY," the doctor said as he squinted at her arm. The tiny ray from his pen flashlight bounced around the wound.

Earlier that day, she'd texted a picture of it to her family—Mom, Dad, two sisters, little brother, sister's fiancé—with the caption: *Does this look like skin cancer?* If that wasn't the perfect example of their warped family dynamic, she didn't know what was—after months of silence and awkward estrangement, she sends a picture of an oozing misshapen sore on a group text, to which they spent the full day trying to diagnose her. It ended with her stoic, emotionless father texting an emoji of a spider.

"It looks like it may be a spider bite," the doctor concluded, clicking off the pen light. "Basal cell usually doesn't itch. I'll give you some cream and we'll go from there. I really don't think it's any type of skin cancer."

She rolled down her sleeve. Guess her dad was right.

She thanked the doctor, took the prescription, and headed out of the building. It figured; she hated going to the doctor and her first visit after a couple years was over a goddamn spider bite. It only further cemented her title of Reluctant Hypochondriac.

Home was a century-old reconstruction they couldn't afford on the top of a hill in the nicest neighborhood around. Even their driveway was grandiose, a long stretch of concrete that made you feel as though you were driving up to a magical castle. The trees were ancient as well, towering above like judgmental giants. *You have the perfect home, the perfect life, why are you so unhappy?* they chastised every time she pulled in.

"It's not skin cancer," she called to her husband as she headed to her office.

"Well, are you dying?" he called back from his, across the hall.

"It's a spider bite."

"Oh, for fuck's sake," he snorted. "Well, sounds like you're stuck with me for a bit longer."

The rest of the day was eventless; piles of laundry, bits of work, kids' homework, dinner, crazy dogs running circles in the living room. She finally settled into bed at eleven or so, absently scratching her arm as she browsed through her phone. She cursed when she noticed the wound had gotten bigger, the big red circle with its oozing middle extending further up her arm. She'd forgotten to pick up the cream from the pharmacy.

That night, she dreamed she was in a dilapidated house with leaking sinks, rainwater pouring down crumbling fireplaces that didn't work. The house was in shambles, puddles of filthy water kicked up by the feral cats and dogs that raced through them. Every hair on her body stood in disgust as she clamped her eyes shut, wondering why the fuck she was raising children in such a mess. How could her husband have picked such a shithole—to save money? When she opened them, there was a spider feasting on her arm.

The next day was exactly the same as the day that preceded it, numb as she listlessly performed the daily dance that was life. Her little brother texted her in jest: *Spider bite sounds cool. Let me know if you suddenly start shooting webs out of your palms.*

The wound was still getting bigger, now taking up the better part of her arm. She'd intended to run to the pharmacy at least a million times, but there was always a distraction, something to sign off on, a runny nose, dog vomit to clean up, a kid that needed to eat. She found some cream around the house and slapped it on, wearing long sleeves so it would stay covered. She had some errands to run tomorrow, she'd pick it up then.

That night, she dreamed of fingers probing her body, tenderly caressing her hidden spaces. She experienced the full moment of bliss in her dream, until she opened her eyes to see a giant, hideous spider above her, dripping poison from its fangs onto her chest. She screamed herself awake, snuggling against the heavy wall that was her husband as she tried to calm her racing heart and ignore the ache between her legs. Her arm itched, but she refused to scratch it.

The next day was a repeat of the thousand before it, this time offering a fresh determination to get the cream. The itching had reached maddening proportions, the lower half of her arm completely red, the sore staring at her like an angry, oozing eye. She tore at it with her fingernails, drawing blood before she wrapped it up with a big Band-Aid. She dropped the kids off at school, stopping to take a quick hike before she headed to the pharmacy.

There was a fragrant breeze in the air, one that reminded her of her teenage years when she thought each day held the promise of a new adventure. She was always a seeker, an explorer, loving life as it was. *Where did that girl go?* she wondered as she stomped through the snow. She loved her family, loved them so much she could burst, and yet...? Where was the adventure life had promised? Somehow she'd lost it, perhaps between Kid Number One and Dog Number Four.

A hawk screeched over head, distracting her. She realized she was scratching her arm through her sweatshirt. It must have been hard, because splotches of scarlet ruined the fabric. She cursed; this was her favorite shirt, one of the few that weren't black. She needed to get that damn cream already.

It was six in the evening when she finally made it to the drugstore down the street. The bespectacled pharmacist told her she needed to come back tomorrow; they had to order it since it was a special kind and it wouldn't be in until then. She nodded, paid for her pack of gum, and headed home.

That night, she wrapped her arm in an old sock so she wouldn't scratch it in her sleep. She drifted off thinking of her childhood, how one night she dreamed a spider was calling her name. She screamed so hard, her mother came racing in. She watched her kill the wolf spider that was sitting behind her nightlight, which had created a giant shadow crawling up the wall.

It was talking to me, she sobbed to her mother.

It was only a dream, her sleep-deprived mother said coldly. *I killed it. Now go back to sleep.*

When she woke, blood and pus had soaked through her makeshift bandage. She unwound it to discover her arm was covered in sores—eight to be exact—spider eyes that gazed at her, adoringly.

"I think I need to go to the hospital," she whispered to the empty spot on the bed. She could hear her husband and the kids downstairs, a typical Saturday morning. She thought of yelling for him, but she doubted he would hear her.

"I don't think I want to get rid of you," she admitted to the eyes.

They seemed to share her sentiment, crying tiny streams of blood onto the bed sheets.

She sighed, listening to the mayhem ensuing downstairs. She should go down there and spend time with them, like a good wife and mother. Then she thought of the mess, the dogs, the sink full of dishes. The world of demands, the pressure to be perfect.

Perhaps she would just stay in bed a bit longer.

The spider in her arm agreed.

THEATRE.

TALIA WOKE IN A FOG. As the haze threaded, she saw dozens of eyes staring down at her, a few more as she looked around the room. Then the pain caught her.

It was silenced by a rush of what could only be laudanum, soothing both discomfort and alarm with a sloppy kiss. Soon the slow drip of blood falling from table to sawdust became a rhythmic, lulling tap that distracted her. It was accompanied by the din of rustling parchment as the long, looming shadows with their faceless eyes adjusted to see her better. The room stank of rotten meat and sweat, and when she turned her head, she saw the blurred shapes of men in aprons crusted by blood splatter. Silver tools laid out on the table glistened in the dim gaslight.

Is this hell? she wondered.

A rat scurried beneath the table she lay on, one of the men stomping it away. When he leaned in to inspect her, his breath smelled of rank tobacco.

Another man, tall with white hair, examined the sharpness of his knife. "Take your positions, gentleman," he said when satisfied. "We have four poor souls today."

"Have you ever seen one of his amputations?" one of the assistants whispered to the other. "'Tis pure artistry."

Talia blinked, still trying to find her way out of the fog. Where was she?

Then she remembered. She'd fainted on the steps of the Howard Manor after months of ignoring the persistent pain that had settled in her bowels, the Howard children screaming in fright. She hadn't wanted to see a doctor, but Mr. Howard insisted she be seen by his friend, the head surgeon at St. Thomas Hospital. She was afraid to lose her employment with the family, so she complied, riding in the carriage with her heart racing and hands clammy. She was terrified of doctors.

Wait, she tried to whisper. *It's my stomach, not my leg.*

"I require silence in the theater," the wizened man ordered, wiping the long blade across his rust-colored apron for good measure.

Dear God, no...

They were already holding her down when she began to scream, realizing what was happening. Their fingers dug into her skin as she thrashed, forcing a stick into her mouth as the surgeon took a deep breath and brought the blade down.

There was no pain, but she heard a loud thud before she fainted, as what could only be her perfectly sound limb hit the straw-covered ground.

Food for the rats.

CATFISH.

SHE CRAWLED INTO BED, the cool breeze tumbling in through her open window. Her friend had warned her about keeping her bedroom window wide open when she lived alone; apparently, that was the way Ted Bundy murdered his victims. Netflix documentaries aside, Kasey had lived alone her entire adult life and was not about to give up the lovely autumn breeze the last few nights had given her. Serial killers be damned.

She took one last peek at her phone, making sure her latest online fling hadn't sent another sexy goodnight text. That was another thing she was consistently chastised over—her penchant for carrying on with strange men over the internet.

"You live alone, Kasey," her friends would cluck. "You're just inviting one of them to stalk or kill you."

She'd shrug. "You only live once."

Tonight, the breeze brought rain, and she drifted off to the pitter-patter of rain on her rooftops.

She woke up to a man's hands around her throat.

He was masked, straddling her to keep her from bucking her hips, his fingers locked around her neck, pressing into the tender flesh. She managed to reach up and snatch off his mask, recognizing her latest Tinder match, a manic glint in his dark eyes. He gnashed his teeth together as he drew black spots in front of her eyes, but she knew if she could just hold on a bit longer; eventually, he would get tired.

"Why aren't you struggling?" he finally asked, exasperated.

She mouthed a reply, causing him to release her.

"What?"

"If you're gonna choke me out, you might as well ride me too," she croaked.

He shook his head incredulously. "You are one sick bitch." He stretched out his fingers while she coughed, ready to try again.

Then he paused, a bewildered look crossing over his handsome face. "What the—?" he murmured, trying to gain his bearings as it became clear he was growing faint.

Kasey coughed again as her regular breathing returned. She wiped the spit from her lips as he collapsed, falling off her bed with a loud thud. She checked her phone to see it was 3 a.m. She sighed. It was going to be a long night.

———

Patrick woke up groggy, pain clawing at his back. His entire world spun, but he slowly put together his surroundings. A flickering fluorescent lamp buzzed above, casting greenish light onto the broken tiles below him. It appeared he was in an abandoned hospital, a table covered in old, dusty papers and plastic tubes within reach.

Somehow, he was looking down from the ceiling. Searing pain followed this revelation, as he soon felt the hooks in his skin that kept him suspended. Panicked, he struggled.

"I wouldn't do that if I were you." A woman slinked into the room, crushing the broken glass scattered around the floor with her heels. He blinked, recognizing the girl he'd met on Writing Twitter, the one he'd come to murder and defile. *That bitch.*

He tried to grab her, but the pain was too much. "Let me go or I'll fucking kill you," he sputtered.

She didn't say a word. Before he could register what was happening, she opened his mouth and ripped out one of his teeth with a pair of pliers. He howled in pain as she chuckled, watching the blood pour into a puddle beneath him. "Next time, it'll be your tongue," she cooed.

He forced himself into silence, seething with rage.

She cocked her head at him as if appreciating her handiwork. "Too bad," she sighed. "You are really handsome, and I loved our banter."

"Please, just—" He couldn't believe he had lowered himself to begging. He'd just had her in his grasp—how had she managed to flip the tables on him?

"Men always think they can overpower women," she explained as if she heard his thoughts. "Which, they often can physically. That's why we have to be smarter." She pulled a vile out of the pocket of her black jeans. "I found out where you lived a while ago and snuck into your apartment. I've been poisoning you slowly over the last few days. I'm delighted you came to me before I could finish, though it meant you weren't as weak as I usually like them before I pounce.

Regardless, I always make sure to lace my windowsill with this before I fall asleep."

The grim reality of Patrick's situation seized him. "Look, please, I'm sorry—"

She reached up and swiftly tore out his tongue.

He was reduced to sobbing, the magnitude of blood loss threatening his consciousness as he stared at the sad hunk of pink on the ground, as it disappeared under the thickening coat of red syrup.

She picked up an ax that had been leaning against the wall, the blade shiny as if brand new. "Isn't this pretty?" she said as she admired it. "I usually torture guys a while first, but I have to work in the morning, and I really wanted to use this. Beheading is fun because the person stays conscious for a few moments after the head is severed."

Patrick found himself praying, unable to do anything else but stare into her eyes. They were illuminated by her triumphant smile as she artfully swung, a loud thud ringing in his ears as the last thing he saw were her stilettos slinking across the floor, trailed by her bloody ax.

THE RISING sun did little to warm the January morning, and I tried not to shiver as I stood at the end of the street waiting for the bus. I shoved my hands into the coat pockets of my winter coat, the one I picked out more for its looks than its practicality, the wind managing to wiggle its way in through the light fabric to my skin. I was grateful to at least be wearing a hat—a fourteen-year-old boy could get away with a hat. It wasn't nearly as pansy-esque as, say, a winter jacket. We had rules to follow, us teen boys.

I sighed, trying to let the grating music that screeched out of my headphones distract me from the frigid weather. It reminded me how badly I needed my driver's license, something to save me from the humiliating ordeal that was waiting for the bus. Still, there were perks. In fact, one of them would be approaching me shortly, I just had to watch out of the corner of my eye.

She finally came around the bend, her eyes cast to the ground as she stomped through the snow with her Doc Martens, barely glancing up behind her fringe of brown hair. I didn't make eye contact. I never did, never even said one word to her, instead standing there, enjoying her presence as we both waited for the creaks and groans signaling the approach of the ancient school bus. If I was lucky, she'd look up, and I'd see a glimpse of her aquamarine eyes before we boarded, perhaps even a polite smile directed my way. I figured maybe one day I'd talk to her, maybe when I had a car. It was hard, though, she seemed as antisocial as me, and we loner types do not like being disturbed.

This wasn't an issue for the next one to join us, a stocky kid with spiked hair named Brad Bryant, whose energy burst the peaceful bubble of loud music and respective distance she and I had created. As much as I didn't want to, I lowered the volume on my MP3 player to hear him.

"What's up, nerd? Listening to that Satanic shit again?" He grinned at Carrie, the object of my adoration, her eyes now fierce as they flew in his direction.

"Fuck off, Bryant."

He laughed. "Someone's PMSing. What's up, Kieve?"

I internally groaned as he came up to clap me on the back. We'd grown up together, two boys the same age living on the same street and all, but I couldn't stand him. We'd clearly gone our separate ways since the days of random football games in the street, him being the sporty jock type with a host of friends, me the quiet loner who'd rather listen to music than socialize. Yet, he didn't give up on me, forcing conversation whenever he could. Honestly, I think he did it to mess with me.

"Think Marilyn Manson over here is PMSing," he

snorted, pointing an elbow toward Carrie, who was clearly trying to ignore both of us.

"Man, just leave her alone," I said before I could help myself. I winced, realizing I'd given him exactly what he wanted.

He feigned a look of shock. "Kieve, my man! You actually like that creepy chick vibe? Hey, man, to each his own—I'm just glad to find out you're not gay."

My cheeks flushed, anger quietly radiating from my stomach and up through my veins. I had a million different retorts, springloaded with a million different ways I could imagine his slow torture and death, but she interrupted.

"Is the bus even coming? It's been more than ten minutes."

We checked our phones to discover she was right.

"Goddamn it, I can't get another tardy, or I'll get fucking detention," Brad groaned.

Before anyone could say anything else, a sound pierced the winter silence, causing Carrie and me to pull off our headphones to listen. It was a distorted, warbling song that reminded me of something they'd play in a cheesy horror flick as the camera pans over to show you the old record player that somehow played by itself. Don Knotts shit.

"What the fuck is an ice cream truck doing out in the dead of winter?" Carrie murmured from beside me, momentarily throwing me off by her close proximity. She smelled like Love Spell and freshly shampooed hair.

The broadcaster of the horrific melody surfaced, a hunk of metal whose peeling paint put our school bus to shame. It creaked and groaned as it hobbled its way through the street sludge, its warped version of *Pop Goes the Weasel* squeaking through its speakers.

The three of us simply stared as it slowed to a halt right in front of us, the song cutting off as the driver rolled down the passenger window.

"Do we look like we want any fucking ice cream?" Brad yelled at the driver.

"Then why are you standing out here?" the driver asked. I squinted but couldn't make out his face in the glaring sun.

"We're waiting for the school bus, you idiot," Brad replied.

"Bus #48 just turned down Peach Street. You missed it."

Brad cursed again and kicked a nearby mailbox. "Fuuuuck, I have a game tonight. I can't get a detention." An idea struck him. "Hey, buddy, can you give us a ride? You're not going to sell any ice cream out here, but I have five bucks."

The driver didn't respond, just hit the unlock button.

Brad grinned, heading towards the hatchback.

"You can't be serious," Carrie sputtered. "You don't know him."

Brad laughed, the loud, obnoxious sound drowning out the sputtering engine of the idling truck. "That creepy old dude ain't gonna do shit. You coming with me, Manson?"

She said nothing, her lovely eyes wider than normal as she shook her head.

"Kieve?"

Carrie's hand clasped around my arm, sending a jolt right through me. "Don't," she warned me. I was cold, tired, annoyed, and definitely not afraid of some old dude in an ice cream truck, but the look in her eyes convinced me.

"Y'all are a bunch of pussies," Brad snorted as he threw open the doors and climbed aboard. His voice echoed in the truck as he yelled, "Hate to break it to you guys, but there's nothing in here but cartons of ice cream."

Carrie did not let go of my arm until the driver put the truck back into drive, summoning that awful sound from the depths of whatever hell it came from, and disappeared around the corner.

"Well, I guess we'd better walk if we want to get to school," I said softly when she didn't move.

She broke free from her stupor, loosening her fingers. "Sorry," she stammered. "I haven't had a bad feeling like that in a long time."

"No worries." I was pleased to discover that talking to her was proving far less terrifying than I'd anticipated, despite the current circumstances.

"If I tell you something, will you promise you won't think I'm nuts?" she asked me, brushing back the messy bangs that fell into her eyes.

I shrugged. "Not really one to judge."

"I'll tell you as we walk," she said, guiding the way.

I wished I was wearing a better coat at this point, but I followed, hoping to warm up during the two-mile walk to school.

She was quiet as if trying to put the right words together. It gave me the opportunity to openly study her, enjoying her pensive face and how her thoughts furrowed her brows and dimpled her nose. She opened her mouth to speak but instead stopped dead in her tracks.

I looked to see what had startled her, observing the same ice cream truck parked and silent on the side of the road. "Guess they didn't make it very far," I commented.

Carrie's face had turned white.

"What's wrong?" I asked.

She wordlessly resumed her march, and I joined her, struck by a sudden apprehension I couldn't explain. Peach Street was a pretty popular road, and it occurred to me that we hadn't seen a car nor another human the entire time we'd been out. Not a single soccer mom van pulled out of a driveway, not one late-to-work car went rushing past.

Carrie's pace slowed as we got closer, heading around to the front to see if the driver was still there.

"He's gone!" she called back.

My eyes settled on the handles on the hatchback, wondering if I should open the doors where we'd last seen Brad. Carrie seemed to read my mind, biting at her lip as she considered the same prospect. We moved in unison, two hands on each handle, ripping open the doors with a loud creak.

I didn't like Brad, not one damn bit, but when I saw him there, splayed out and held in place by rope, his skin torn from his muscles and hooked so all his muscles were exposed, I almost joined Carrie as she vomited her coffee and what looked like muffin into the snow. I had trouble tearing my eyes away, wondering what it felt like to be flayed, shuddering as I noted the skin had been evenly peeled and kept intact, meaning his final moments were spent in utter agony. Carrie's arm grabbed mine.

"We have to go before it gets back," she said frantically.

"When what gets back?"

But then I heard a screech in the distance, an other-worldly pitch that rivaled the scream of a hawk.

She and I ran as fast as we could from the truck, moving from house to house to fruitlessly pound on each door. Finally, I grabbed her arm, pulling her back towards my house as the screeching intensified.

I knew my back door was always left open, and as I pulled her towards it, she slipped on a patch of ice, hitting the ground hard. She scrambled back to her feet, a patch of snow darkened by her split lip. I ran to help her just as something loomed behind her.

It was the size of a large human, but that was where the comparisons ended. Each finger and toe ended in long, razor claws, its skin red and leathery like Brad's poor mutilated corpse. Its eyes were like peeled grapes, pupilless but seeing as it lurched to-wards us, a bifurcated tongue slipping out from a wall of crooked, sharpened teeth. It smelled of old fish and spoiled milk.

"Heat," Carrie screamed, trying to pull my atten-tion back onto her. "It hates heat!"

I didn't even pause to question it, grabbing the lighter out of my pocket to give it a flick.

The creature stepped back, narrowing its eyes as its tail twitched with agitation.

Carrie was shaking, but she opened my backpack and pulled out one of my notebooks. She tore the pages, using her own lighter to set them ablaze. The creature backed off but continued to watch us as if knowing we'd soon run out of paper.

She and I edged back toward my house as I tried to devise a plan. I wondered how I would tell Carrie; if the creature could understand our words if I tried.

Fortunately, she didn't need an explanation, trusting me enough to follow me to the garage. I slammed the door shut just as the creature, with no fire to deter it, slammed into it, scratching at the glass window with its claws.

Although the sound it made was earsplitting, I didn't falter. I was no longer in control of my body; sheer adrenaline had taken the reins, knowing there were only moments before the creature broke through. I grabbed the garage door opener out of the sports car my dad kept covered in the winter and tossed it to Carrie. Then I grabbed the bottle of lighter fluid from the top shelf and doused the car and as much of the inside as I could. I caught her eyes and gave her a slow nod.

She pressed the garage door opener as I chucked my lighter at the car, the small explosion immediately sparking flame. The creature flew in through the opened door just in time to be blasted with building fire while Carrie and I raced out the side door. We covered our ears against its frantic screeching until it dwindled to a low hiss and then, to nothing.

We collapsed in the snow, catching our breath as we watched the flames swallow my dad's garage. How the hell was I going to explain this to him? I wondered.

I turned to Carrie, who wiped the blood from her lip, the fire reflected in her eyes.

"What was that thing?" I asked her.

"We're not in the real world anymore," she said, matter-of-factly and slightly dismayed. "That's not the last of them either."

I bolted upright. "What do you mean?"

She sighed, pulling herself to her feet. She brushed

the snow off her dark jeans. "Come on. We need to find more weapons and a place to rest. It's going to be a long night."

I stared at her, mystified until she helped me up. "How do you know all this?"

"This is not my first rodeo," she sighed, pulling me to my feet. "So trust me when I say we need to go now."

No sooner had she spoken than we heard the awful melody of an ice cream truck as it turned down our street. Carrie promptly ran, but I was frozen, staring with horror at the driver who waved to me, wearing Brad's face.

LEMONADE.

"THOSE KIDS ARE GOING to get kidnapped," her high-pitched voice echoed in the foyer. "No parent in their right mind would allow their children to sit on the corner like that."

Craig was tired. It had been way too long of a day for this. He slipped off his shoes at the door, yearning to get past her to reach the refrigerator and its collection of imported beers hidden in the back. "Honey, it's a lemonade stand. We used to do things like that all the time when we were kids."

"It was different back then," his wife insisted, putting her hands on her hips. "It's a scary world out there."

"We live in a wealthy suburb, Laura."

"But they're at the end of the development, right by a major intersection! Anyone coming down 82 can stop, snatch them up, and drive away. I'm calling their parents."

"Alright, alright." Craig sighed and put his shoes back on. "I'll go talk to them, okay? Just put the phone down."

The neighborhood was quiet, free of the typical background noise of roaring lawnmowers and kids playing in their front yards. He wondered if the residents of Treeflower Lane even mowed their own grass—since they'd moved into their new McMansion at 8614, he'd yet to see one do it. It's funny how things like the sound of obnoxious lawnmowers are what one becomes accustomed to and how its absence can breed nostalgia. He shook his head. They had been so excited when he first got the promotion, but it turned out that life was still just as big a pain in the ass as it was pre-brand-new-big-house-in-a-ritzy-development-with-a-good-school-system. Their problems were just more expensive.

He squinted in the setting sun to see the two young kids up ahead, seated behind their picnic table, their little hands folded, watching the cars pass them by with big innocent eyes. He was sad to see their jar held only a couple of coins, their pitcher of lemonade far from empty. Guess the rich people around here didn't want any lemonade.

As he got closer, he realized they were the Brooks kids, and suddenly, it all made sense. Tom Brooks inherited his parent's house and immediately moved in, even though he was an auto mechanic at the nearby Shell station who worked extra shifts at the oil change place on the weekends. Craig had met him when his kids were out making a snowman without boots, his wife horrified to see their reddening skin above their sneakers. He seemed a nice enough guy, just very distracted. He felt for him—he couldn't imagine raising two kids as a single father.

The rest of the neighborhood did not feel the same way, treating them like an abomination that had no part among the neatly manicured lawns and Homeowners Association-approved mailboxes. His heart broke for them—he couldn't even imagine what school must be like alongside the most spoiled kids the nearby counties had to offer.

Craig reached into his pockets, grateful he had a few dollars stashed away with the single-serving packs of nicotine gum. "Hello," he greeted them as he pushed the bills into their jar. "I'd like a cup of lemonade, please."

The little girl—he couldn't remember her name for the life of him—eyed the crumpled bills at the bottom of the jar. "A cup is only 25 cents."

The little boy—his name had to be Max, Craig was sure of it—pointed to their cardboard sign that read, FRESH LEMONADE - 25 CENTS!

Craig shrugged. "It's a tip."

The little girl accepted his excuse and hurried to get him a cup, sloshing the liquid all over the grass as she did so.

"Careful, you're going to waste it," Maybe Max warned her.

"It's okay," Craig assured them. "How long have you guys been out here? It's got to be close to dinner time."

Maybe Max shrugged. "Dad's working late tonight."

Craig knew his wife would kill him if he invited them over for supper, but she would also kill him if he didn't get them off the street. "Why don't you guys let me get you some McDonald's? I'd invite you to accompany me, but I don't want to be that creepy stranger who invites kids into his car."

The little girl laughed as she handed him his cup.

"We know who you are, Mr. Talbot. You live across the street. My name is Cyndi, by the way."

"Cyndi, that's right." Craig nodded as he sipped the lemonade. It was surprisingly cold and refreshing, with just enough sugar to soothe the tartness without hurting your teeth. He was genuinely impressed.

"It's a recipe our grandma gave us," Maybe Max told him. "We'll go with you to McDonald's. Come on, Cyndi, just grab the money."

Craig was grateful his driveway was long enough and his house big enough that his wife didn't hear him as he snuck up and took the car. The kids settled quietly into the backseat, putting on their seat belts without any fuss. Such good kids, he thought to himself as he pulled out of their development and headed up the street to McDonald's. They didn't even demand shakes or Big Macs, even when Craig waved away their earnings and assured them he could afford whatever they wanted. They were content sipping on their Sprites with a hamburger and small fries each on their laps.

He and Laura had tried for children when they first married, but after rounds of treatments, trials, and experiments, they'd finally decided to try life as a childless couple. Sometimes he wondered if that was why she was so centered in on children that weren't hers, her maternal instincts pushing to break free. Craig had accepted it, but if he were to have kids, he hoped they'd be like the Brooks kids.

"Thanks for the food, Mr. Talbot," Maybe Max said as the car grew closer to their street. "I was hoping you'd finally take us out of there before the explosion."

"Explosion?" Craig looked at him in the rear-view mirror.

"Yeah, you know, the one that kills us," Cyndi replied with her mouth full.

Craig suddenly felt a wave of unease behind the steering wheel. "Are you guys messing with me?"

He saw them look at each other before Maybe Max shifted uncomfortably in his seat. "I'm sorry, Mr. Talbot, we thought you were remembering. That's why you came to save us."

"Listen, kiddo, I was just helping you guys out with a bite to eat," he told them. "I don't know about any explosion—" He brought the car to a screeching halt when he realized their street was missing, grateful there weren't any other cars sharing the road when he swerved, parking it on the grass. "Did I make a wrong turn somewhere…?"

He looked around him. The main street was still the same. The trees were still the same. But their development was gone. There was no road, no houses, no signs, no lamps. Nothing. Just a lemonade stand.

Frantic, he looked at the kids sitting silently in the backseat. "What is going on?" he demanded.

Maybe Max bit his lip uncomfortably, and Cyndi's wide brown eyes bore into his. She decided to be the one to speak, "Dad, you really don't remember?"

Craig started to tremble, wanting very badly to get out of his car and go somewhere—go anywhere, go home…but there was no home. "Remember what?" he whispered in a voice that didn't feel like his.

"We wanted to set up a lemonade stand outside, but Mom wouldn't let us," Max said gently. "So we were there when the house exploded. She was at the grocery store."

Craig's mouth went dry, his nose overwhelmed by the smell of gasoline.

"We were hoping one day you would come with us," Cyndi said. "But you never want to leave. Max and I have been trying to get your attention, but nothing has ever worked. Until Max came up with the lemonade stand idea. He said you'd come if it's a lemonade stand."

Craig stared at his son, speechless, noticing the thick waves of sandy brown hair he'd inherited from his mother were in patches.

"Come on, Dad," he said gently. "It's time to go."

Craig looked back at the woods where his development had just been, the development they'd never lived in, wondering if he'd ever get the scent of burned wood and plastic out of his clothes. He suddenly felt peaceful, glad he'd gotten the kids something to eat even though his weekend shifts at Reddi Oil were getting cut short and money was tight again. A few droplets of blood fell onto the dash as he adjusted his rear-view mirror, smiling at the kids with grinning skulls and charred skin sitting in the backseat.

"Make sure you don't leave the wrappers on the floor," he told them as he put the car in drive.

"We won't," Max promised.

Craig suddenly remembered his paper Dixie cup sitting in the center console and took a long sip. There really was nothing quite like fresh, sweet lemonade.

ON THE THIRD DAY, I stopped screaming.

Up until the day the Devil came to call, I kept my nails modestly trimmed. When I awoke in his hell, they'd grown into claws.

I can no longer determine if I'm alive or dead, but I think I was once a young woman with chestnut hair and a waist narrow enough to forgo a corset. I cannot remember my name. All I can remember is crimson-stained skirts splayed out in the sun and the smell of sharp, metallic bile piercing the sultry summer heat.

Did I tell you of my nails? They stare back at me now, embedded in the ceiling of this rotting chamber I am trapped in. I wish I could tell the preachers Hell is not fire and ash as they preached, but cold, damp, breathless air. The echo of horse hooves you cannot see. Voices you can barely hear.

I did try, you know. Not to end up here. I cannot remember my name or the color of my eyes, but I remember how badly I tried to be good.

Perhaps it's because of the time I stood on child tiptoes to peer over the ledge, watching them shuffle along Factors Walk. Heard their chains drag along the brick as I thought, *thank God it's not me.*

Hellfire is a sham; I miss Savannah swelter. I miss moss swinging from the old oak trees and the hum of tree frogs. The heat that three cold baths cannot fix and the scream of crickets at the height of summer, warning all to stay indoors. Anything but this shivering, dank prison.

I deserve it, I suppose.

For why else would I exist now, in this space?

The last full memory I have is of her face, my beloved Grace, who caught me when I fell in the second-floor privy. "You have the fever..." she whispered, her voice rattled with fear.

Then it was dark, then it was this, and now, I wonder how much longer I will exist.

ACKNOWLEDGEMENTS.

To my peers in my writing classes, who read my stories with a mixture of confusion, horror, and intrigue, thank you.

To my faithful readers who have put up with my antics throughout the years and still buy my books, thank you.

To every soul at Quill & Crow Publishing House for helping me keep the lights on while yelling at me to rest and write, thank you.

To Damon Barret Roe, for her sharp editing eye and giving me the Rho special for this collection, thank you.

To my boys for their constant inspiration ("Mom, you should write a story like THIS!"), thank you and I love you.

To my husband who, after all these years, is still my biggest fan and source of encouragement, thank you and I love you.

And to anyone who took the time to read this book, thank you from the bottom of my little black heart.

ABOUT THE AUTHOR.

Gothic horror writer Cassandra L. Thompson has been creating stories since she got her grubby little hands around a pen. When she is not busy managing a house full of feral children (human and canine) with her beloved husband, you can find her wandering around cemeteries, taking pictures of abandoned things, or in the library researching her latest obsession. She has a B.A. in History and an MLIS, but she ignores her degrees to focus on writing and running Quill & Crow Publishing House, both of which require copious amounts of coffee and Crows.

For new stories and to stay up-to-date on all happenings, join the Mother of Crows newsletter on Substack. If you enjoy Gothic horror/dark fantasy, please check out **The Ancient Ones Trilogy**, available through your favorite retailers.

THANK YOU FOR READING.

Thank you for reading *My Little Black Book of Horror*. We deeply appreciate our readers, and are grateful for everyone who takes the time to leave us a review. If you're interested, please visit our website to find review links. Your reviews help small presses and indie authors thrive, and we appreciate your support.

The Crow Collections

1 Ending in Ashes

#3 Changes (2024)

#4 Mirth & Malice: Scenes from the Sideshow (2025)

#5 Bury Me Cold & Other Last Words (2025)

insects.

Slugger.

domestic abuse, drug addiction, graphic patricide.

Soulmates.

assisted suicide, suicide, self-harm.

Theatre.

medical malpractice, medical trauma, amputation.

Broken.

mental illness, amputation, alcoholism.

Push.

murder, potential child kidnapping.

Catfish.

graphic murder.

Monsters.

graphic murder, skinning, creature horror.

Lemonade.

death of loved ones / children, poverty.

Alive.

buried alive, implied slavery.

9 781958 228463